Edward Walford

William Pitt

A Biography

Edward Walford

William Pitt
A Biography

ISBN/EAN: 9783337098810

Printed in Europe, USA, Canada, Australia, Japan

Cover: Foto ©Raphael Reischuk / pixelio.de

More available books at **www.hansebooks.com**

WILLIAM PITT:

A Biography.

BY

EDWARD WALFORD, M.A.,

FORMERLY SCHOLAR OF BALLIOL COLLEGE, OXFORD;

Author of
"The County Families," "The Windsor Peerage," etc.

LONDON:
CHATTO & WINDUS, 214, PICCADILLY.
1890.

CONTENTS.

 CONTENTS.

CHAPTER VII.

CHAPTER VIII.

CHAPTER IX.

CHAPTER X.

CHAPTER XI.

CHAPTER XII.

CHAPTER XIII.

CONTENTS. vii

THE LIFE OF PITT.

CHAPTER I.

*Introductory—Old and Later Whigs and Tories
—Lord Russell on Pitt's Policy.*

IT is to be feared that although the lot ot
William Pitt was cast in an age which was
critical and eventful to a high degree, and
therefore one which must interest every
Englishman, yet the same can scarcely be
said of the biography of him who was the
ruler of the destinies of this country for the
last twenty years of the last century and
for the first few years of this. Mr. Pitt's
life itself was uneventful, and he himself
did not pour out his soul to his friends in

B

letters, or post up a diary day by day. In fact, there are few men who let their acquaintances, and much more the world around them, so little into their secrets; and therefore it has been well remarked that his biography, however ably written, " must lack much of that picturesqueness, and much also of the passion, which interests the majority of readers." To quote Mr. Kebbel's own words: " Pitt was a minister as far removed above the intrigues of common statesmen as above the intellects of common men. In private life he betrayed none of those frailties which, however deplorable in a hero, make a biography more interesting by widening the circle within which mysteries can be bred and public curiosity be sustained. Whether as a man or as a minister, he stood out in singularly bold relief before the public eye. He had no secrets, either political or social. When he came into power, he came in because he was necessary to Government, not because Government was necessary to him. . . . There has probably never been a Prime Minister of this country who answers so completely to the idea conveyed by the popular phrase of being 'above board.'"[1]

But, on the other hand, there is comfort to be found for the writer who is bold enough to undertake such a task as his biography. The main outlines of his public life at least, and some few portions of his private life, are no sealed book. He lived for the last twenty years of his existence under the bright light which beats down not only on thrones, but on Ministries and Cabinets. His life, at least ever since he reached his majority, is interwoven with that of the country which he served, and of which he was so justly proud. Almost as soon as he was of legal age he entered Parliament, and scarcely had he taken his seat in the House of Commons when he was called to join the Administration, and to take office, first as Chancellor of the Exchequer, and then as Prime Minister. In the words of his biographer, Gifford : "Fortunately for the historian, the circumstances and transactions of Mr. Pitt's ad-

[1] "Essays on History and Politics," by T. E Kebbel, p. 137.

ministration are not locked up in the Cabinet, or confined within the bosom of any individual: they have all been subjected to public analysis and submitted to public discussion. He was, in fact, the historian of his own measures, the expounder of his own principles, and the herald of his own deeds. Mr. Pitt's actions required no subterfuge to disguise and no artifice to conceal them. . . . With the pride of conscious integrity he solicited investigation and courted publicity. In his luminous and comprehensive speeches in Parliament he has explained his motives and unfolded his views, objects, and designs, and has thus, by the supply of an invaluable fund of materials, greatly facilitated the labours of his political biographer."

It will also doubtless be a disappointment to some readers to find that in the following pages William Pitt, who is popularly identified with the Tory party and with the special friends and favourites of King George III., is not treated in a partisan spirit. Though he inherited from his father some of the traditions of the Whigs under the two first Georges, yet, like that father, he stood personally aloof from, or rather superior to, party and party ties. The fact is that in his natural instincts he was true to both the King and the people, and that he desired to legislate in the interests of both, and so to maintain that equipoise in our constitution which, if Aristotle is to be accepted as an authority, is the preservation of a State.[1] It is true that in the second period of his long tenure of the Premiership (1793–1800) he departed to some extent from the public advocacy of those advanced opinions which he held and maintained in his earlier days ; but that departure arose less from a change of political opinions in the abstract than from a conviction that there are times when it is wise to keep in abeyance questions which are not likely to be widely dealt with in certain circumstances, or, to use a phrase widely current in his day, that "it is not good to repair one's buildings in the hurricane season." To this extent, it must be

[1] Τὸ ἀντιπεπονθὸς σώζει τὰς πολιτείας. Pol., B. ii. chap. 9.

allowed that Mr. Pitt was a renegade from those enlightened principles which he advocated firmly under a narrow-minded and despotic sovereign ; and thus far we cannot refuse to go along with Professor Goldwin Smith when he writes of the younger William Pitt that he was "not one person, but two."

Accordingly in the following pages the reader, perhaps, will notice the almost total absence of the terms "Whig" and "Tory." And the reason is not far to seek. In the course of a century terms come to change their meaning by the course of events; and it is often said, with as much truth as wit, that the Whigs of to-day are the Tories of to-morrow. Lord Stanhope, in his History of England, states that in Queen Anne's reign the relative meaning of the two terms "Whig" and "Tory" was not only different, but opposite to that which they bore at the accession of William IV. "The main principle of each, no doubt, continued the same, the leading principle of the Whigs being the dread of Royal encroachment, while the leading principle of the Tories was the dread of popular licentiousness. The same person who in 1712 would have been a Whig would probably have been a Tory in 1830. For on examination it will be found that, in nearly all particulars, a modern Tory resembled a Whig of Queen Anne's reign, and a Tory of Queen Anne's reign was not unlike a modern Whig."

And what were the principles of the Whig party a century ago? The answer is not difficult to find. At the termination of the American War the new Whigs attempted to bring about political reforms and changes of which the old Whigs had not thought. These schemes had for their objects the acknowledgment of American independence and the granting of political equality to Ireland ; the promotion of religious liberty, parliamentary reform, and the liberty of the press, which up to that time had been in shackles. " Had these principles prevailed from 1770 to 1820," writes Lord Russell, " this country would have avoided the American War and the first revolutionary war, the rebellion of 1798 in Ireland, and the creation of three or four hundred millions of National Debt." How far such surmises would have been verified by Mr. Pitt's history, had his life been prolonged, the reader will be perhaps more able to judge when he has studied the following chapters of the present narrative.

Lord Russell appears to me to " hit the right nail on the head " on this subject in his " Recollections," which contain a brief retrospect of the reign of George III., and a general survey of his ministers. He reminds us that it was Pitt who, first as a private member and afterwards as a minister, brought forward almost the first proposals for a reform of the House of Commons, and concluded the first commercial treaty with France that was based on the principles of free trade ; that it was Pitt, not his antagonist Fox, who had proclaimed that Scotland and Ireland ought to be placed on a footing of equality with England ; and that he projected the admission of Roman Catholics to seats in the legislature, and the permanent endowment of the Roman Catholic clergy, though

he did not live to carry out either project.
But he also reminds us that it was through
"playing on the fears of England" at the
outbreak of the French Revolution, and
through the first ten years of the war with
the great Napoleon, that Pitt raised the
National Debt from a hundred and thirty
to eight hundred millions ; and he excuses
Pitt's departure in middle life from the
honest convictions of his youth on the
ground of the "imminent perils of the
war itself, and the necessity of combining
the elements of a majority who might
agree on the policy of continuing the war,
although they might differ upon all other
questions." If this be so, then we cannot
acquit the great minister from the charge
of postponing his zeal for reform, and of
putting free trade and justice to Ireland in
abeyance, partly in deference to what he
called the " Jacobin " party, and partly out
of too great deference to the wishes of the
king, and the strong religious scruples
which disturbed his mind with regard to
his coronation oath. "Had," he writes,
"Pitt lived till 1815, he might have re-

curred to his study of Adam Smith, and promoted freedom of trade with foreign countries ; he might have introduced a temperate reform of the representation ; he might have pacified Ireland without waiting for the threat of civil war, or fearing the conscientious scruples of the Prince Regent." [1]

But it is idle to speculate on what would or might have happened if such and such conditions had only been fulfilled ; and upon such points different minds will form different estimates. We can judge men only by their actions while they are free to act ; and there can be little doubt in the minds of Englishmen that William Pitt's freedom of action came to an end with the outbreak of the French Revolution, or at all events that he thought such to be the case, which comes pretty much to the same thing practically.

[1] " Recollections of Earl Russell," p. 23.

CHAPTER II.

The Pitt Family—Heredity—Pitt's Birth and Childhood—His Education—His Delicate Health—Life at Burton Pynsent.

THE Pitt family, from which the Earl of Chatham and his son were sprung, according to Sir Bernard Burke and the heralds, can be traced up to Nicholas Pitt, who was living in the reign of Henry VI., and whose grandson, John Pitt, was Clerk of the Exchequer under one of the Tudors. This John Pitt had three sons, of whom the eldest, Sir William, Comptroller of the Household and a principal officer of the Exchequer under James I., was the ancestor of the Pitts of Stratfieldsaye, Hampshire, whose representative in 1776 was raised to the peerage as Lord Rivers of Stratfieldsaye, a title which became extinct in 1828. His second son, another

John, settled in Ireland ; whilst the third
son, Thomas, who resided at Blandford, in
Dorsetshire, being appointed, in the reign
of Queen Anne, Governor of Fort St.
George, in the East Indies, was the
fortunate purchaser of the celebrated Pitt
diamond, which weighed 127 carats, and
by the sale of which to the Regent of
France he made a profit of nearly
£115,000.   He subsequently was Governor
of Jamaica, and, returning in middle age
to England, sat in four Parliaments as
M.P., first for Old Sarum, and secondly for
Thirsk.   At his death in 1726 he was
buried in Blandford St. Mary Church,
where a large marble monument, with a
long Latin inscription, records his memory.
"Governor" Pitt's second son, Thomas,
married an Irish heiress, and was created
Earl of Londonderry in Ireland ; but the
title lasted for only two generations.   His
third and youngest son John, M.P., and an
officer in the army, married a daughter of
Lord Fauconberg, who, strangely enough,
was a connection of Oliver Cromwell's
family.   His two daughters married re-

spectively James, first Earl Stanhope, and Mr. Charles Cholmondeley, of Vale Royal, a Cheshire squire, whose descendant in the fourth generation is now Lord Delamere.

Meantime Robert, the eldest son of "Governor" Pitt, had bought the fine estate of Boconnoc, near Lostwithiel, in the south of Cornwall, where he settled down as a country squire. He was a member of the House of Commons, and one of the clerks of the Board of Green Cloth, and he married the sister of John Villiers, Earl of Grandison in the Irish peerage. He, however, enjoyed his property but a few short months, for he followed his father to the grave after an interval of little more than a year. He left two sons, Thomas, his successor at Boconnoc (the father of another Thomas, afterwards created Lord Camelford), and William, "the great Commoner" of the reign of George II., who became Earl of Chatham by creation, and was the father of the statesman whose life is recorded in these pages. When George III. ascended the throne of Great Britain, in the autumn of 1760, the younger William Pitt was an infant in his mother's nursery at Hayes, near Beckenham, in Kent. The elder Pitt was at that time in the prime of manhood, and in the full glory of his public career, and he had lately purchased his pleasant rural retreat of Hayes out of the savings of his salary as a minister of the Crown. There he consoled himself in the midst of his public labours by laying out his grounds and planting those trees which it was the fate of strangers to enjoy, for his eldest son sold the estate almost as soon as he inherited it.

At Hayes, then, William, the second son of "the great Commoner," first saw the light on the 28th of May, 1759. He was born, Lord Stanhope tells us, "in the best bedroom, probably the same in which his father died." He seems from his infancy to have been his parents' favourite, probably in part on account of his extreme precocity, but partly also for another reason, which shall be mentioned presently. "The year 1759," writes Lord Stanhope,

" was perhaps the most glorious and eventful in his father's life. The impulse given to the war by that great orator and statesman was apparent in unexampled victories obtained in every quarter of the globe. In Germany we gained the battle of Minden ; in North America we gained the battle of Quebec. In Africa we reduced Goree, and in the West Indies Guadeloupe. In the East we beat back the son of the Emperor of Delhi, and the chiefs of the Dutch at Chinsura. Off the coast of Brittany we prevailed in the great naval conflict of Quiberon ; off the coast of Portugal, in the great naval conflict of Lagos. Indeed —so Horace Walpole, at the close of this year complains, in a letter to Sir Horace Mann—'one is forced to ask every morning what victory there is, for fear of missing one.' "[1] There can be little doubt that the birth of this son thus coinciding with the acme of his fortune and fame, made him all the more dear to his proud paternal heart.

---

[1] " Life of Pitt," vol. i. p. 2.

As a child, he learned with ease and rapidity; and as he passed into boyhood, his remarks are said to have shown a sagacity and wisdom far in advance of his years. He was by no means strong in his physique; and hence he was not sent to school, but was handed over to the care of a governess, and afterwards of a private tutor, the Rev. Edward Wilson, who subsequently became, by favour of his grateful pupil, a canon of Westminster.

After all, however, he owed the greatest part of his early education to his father, who taught him the art of oratory in a practical way, by making him stand on a stage and recite speeches on historical questions, and afterwards write long essays, in which he discussed their "pros" and their "cons," after the manner of the politicians of the day.

Near the entrance to the stable yard at Hayes Place is still shown a stone step or horse-block, which is said to have been put there by the great Lord Chatham for his boys to mount their ponies. A tradition of the place runs to the effect that the father used to make his son William mount this stone for another purpose also; namely, as a rostrum, standing on which he taught him to deliver speeches on historical and political subjects, thus training him in the arts of Parliamentary elocution. The elder Pitt was a consummate orator, so that he could hardly have failed to make a good practical teacher. Thus trained under so accomplished a tutor as his father in an art which few boys at that period were taught, it is little wonder that the son proved himself an apt disciple, and that he soon distanced all his fellows. He was brought up mainly at Hayes, and at Burton Pynsent, near Langport, in Somerset, a mansion and estate which had been left to the Earl by an eccentric baronet, Sir William Pynsent, as a token of the admiration which he felt for him as a public man. The Pitt family settled down at Burton Pynsent, it would appear, when Willy Pitt was about six years old.

The house is still standing, in part at least, and it belongs to Col. W. Pinney, formerly M.P. for Lyme and for West

Somerset ; but it is to a great degree dis-
mantled, and a farmer occupies that part
which was added by Lord Chatham. The
house stands about $3\frac{1}{2}$ miles from Langport
station. The dimensions of the rooms
built by Lord Chatham are given at length
in Collinson's " History of Somerset " ; and
in the park near the house is a lofty monument, which Lord Chatham erected to the
memory of Sir William Pynsent. His
lordship was very fond of the northern and
eastern views, as seen from the windows ;
the former view embraced the battle-field
of Sedgmoor, and the room which commands it was " the Library " ; the other
room, looking to the east, was called the
" Bird Room." It is almost needless to
add that, in spite of the fine growth of the
timber trees which surround it, the house
wears an appearance of desolation, when
compared with what it was some hundred
and thirty years ago.

Throughout his boyhood, William Pitt's
health continued to cause anxiety ; at all
events, his father writes thus to his medical
attendant, Dr. Addington, in August, 1771,

from Burton Pynsent: "I wish I could say of our dear William that he is mended since you saw him. His neck is rather less, but he is wan and extremely lean— in other respects not ill." And again in November: "Our dear William has held out well on the whole, but lately has had again a disturbed night. The blister was applied, and he is, thank God, well at present. We trust that confection and airing in a carriage will keep him so." Again later, "My poor boy William is still ailing." Such, writes Lord Stanhope, is the constant burden of the father's letters during his boyhood. There were great fears that so frail a plant would never be reared to full maturity.

Of his boyhood but few stories are related. Lord Stanhope tells us that when he was only seven years old he said: "I am glad that I am not the eldest son, as I want to speak in the House of Commons, like papa." He also records, though with some doubt of its authenticity, a saying of Lady Holland, the mother of Charles James Fox, that "Willy Pitt, though not eight years old, was the cleverest child she ever saw, and a prophecy that he would be a thorn in her son's side as long as he lived." From a more trustworthy source, the "Memoirs" of his early friend, and his successor in the Premiership, the Right Honourable Henry Addington, afterwards Lord Sidmouth, we learn that the young Pitts took part, as children, in some private theatrical performances at Hayes, at which young Addington was present as an invited guest and spectator, the great Earl of Chatham, their father, being prompter and stage-manager; and that, in spite of his parental fondness for his second son, he owned that Willy was "an awkward youth, and acquitted himself with remarkable stiffness." It is clear, therefore, that he was not born to shine as a light in the same hemisphere with David Garrick.

As young Pitt grew up to boyhood, he showed many tokens of a mind mature beyond his years. Thus, in April, 1772, Lady Chatham writes to her husband: "The fineness of Willy's mind makes him enjoy with the highest pleasure what would be above the reach of any other creature of his small age." And in the following year the poet Hayley, who was staying at Lyme at the same time with young Pitt, describes him as "a wonderful boy of fourteen," and in his "Memoirs" speaks of the pleasure which he even then derived from the conversation of his young acquaintance; adding his regret that owing to shyness and reserve he did not himself impart to "the wonderful youth" an epic poem which he had lately begun.

"But even at this period," Lord Stanhope tells us, "Willy Pitt had himself become a poet. He had written a tragedy in five acts, and in blank verse, entitled 'Laurentius, King of Clarinium.' It was privately acted at Burton Pynsent in August, 1772, and again in the following year. The prologue was spoken by Mr. Pitt, and the actors were himself and his brothers and sisters. Lord Macaulay mentions it in his well-known essay on Pitt, as "not worse than the tragedies of Hayley," and as being "in some respects highly curious. There is no love. The whole plot is political ; and it is remarkable that the interest, such as it is, turns on a contest about a Regency. On the one side is a faithful servant of the Crown, on the other an ambitious and unprincipled conspirator. At length the king, who had been missing, reappears, resumes his power, and rewards the faithful defender of his rights." It may be added that the MS. of this play is still carefully preserved at Lord Stanhope's seat, Chevening, near Sevenoaks.

At this time Mr. Wilson's tuition was still superintended by the watchful eye of his father, who, unless ill, never allowed a day to pass without giving instruction of some sort or other to his children, and seldom without reading with them a chapter of the Bible.

In spite of ill-health, and the frequent interruption of his studies which it entailed, so apt a scholar did Willy prove, that, while still a lad, he had mastered most of the classical authors then read at public schools, and the elements of mathematics besides. His tutor once observed of him that he seemed never to learn, but only to recollect.

"At fourteen he was as forward as most lads at seventeen or eighteen, and was considered already ripe for college." By his father's recommendation he read Barrow's Sermons for style, and for that *verborum copia* which is so necessary to an orator ; and, at his suggestion, he was taken by Mr. Wilson at Cambridge through a course of Thucydides, Polybius, and Quinctilian. He entered on residence at Pembroke College in that University in 1773, when he was little more than fourteen.

CHAPTER III.

College Life at Cambridge—Removal to London —Takes Chambers in Lincoln's Inn—Life in West-End Circles—" Goosetree's" Club— Pitt's Social Habits and Early Friends.

HAD Willy Pitt as a boy been sent, like his father before him, to Eton, he would probably have become an adept in writing Latin verses with elegance and grace ; but, even without this advantage, he showed himself an accomplished classical scholar, though when he grew to manhood, and entered Cambridge, his taste was developed more fully in the direction of mathematical than of classical studies.

Inheriting, however, from his father a profound contempt for any other laurels than those to be won in the arena of public life and as a member of the Legislature, it does not appear that he offered himself a candidate for the honours of the Mathematical Tripos, at that time almost the only test of University distinction.

The details of William Pitt's college life are scanty in the extreme; all we know is that, according to the fashion with young men of family at that time, he was accompanied, when he went into residence at Cambridge, by his tutor, Mr. Wilson; and it appears that his father indulged him with a horse, probably in order to enable his son to keep himself at once in good health, and also select in his company, and to save him from associating with young men of the vulgar herd.

Soon after entering on residence at Cambridge he had a serious illness, and for two months was confined to his rooms; and consequently he was obliged to remain at home for the first half of the following year. He was placed under the care of his father's friend, Dr. Addington; and by his advice he took daily draughts of port wine, at the same time abstaining from the bad habit of reading late at night. After this he not only had no relapse, but became a fairly healthy man, and he continued to remain such for many years.

He took his Bachelor's degree from Pembroke College in 1776 without passing any examination, as was the custom for the sons of noblemen ; and he must have established his fame for superior powers very firmly as an undergraduate, for he had no sooner taken his degree than we find him not only looking forward to senatorial honours, but even thinking of contesting the representation of his University with men far his seniors and already in possession. This is the more surprising seeing that in his day there was at Cambridge no "Union" or other Debating Society in which he could have exhibited the results of his father's early training.

His career at the University would seem to have been marked by the very strictest morals, and his after-life did not depart from them. Indeed, so remarkable was the strictness of his life, that it was a favourite taunt against him with the young wits and "bloods" at Brook's, as though a chaste life were a disgrace.

The monotony of his residence at Cambridge had been varied, however, by occasional journeys to London. He generally took care to be in town whenever his father was about to bring forward any important motion, or to make any great speech in the House of Peers ; and his letters to his mother at this date usually describe some details of the debate. His elder and his younger brother being both absent abroad, it fell to his lot, along with his brother-in-law, Lord Mahon, to support Lord Chatham on that day when, with the hand of death already upon his frame, he went for the last time to the House of Lords to raise his voice in the cause of his country. Aided by some of his brother peers, the two bore him into an adjoining chamber, and thence followed him to Hayes, where he died a month afterwards.

I have dwelt at greater length on Pitt's early education and youth because in him "the child was" eminently "the father of the man," and because "it is surely no less consonant to the laws of nature and reason than to those of the Homeric poems that the arming of the hero for the battle should enter into the description of the battle itself, or at all events should lead up to it." [1]

At the public funeral of his father in Westminster Abbey, owing to the absence of his elder brother abroad, he walked as chief mourner, supported by Mr. Thomas Pitt, of Boconnoc, the head of the family, and by his brother-in-law, Lord Mahon. On the same day he writes to his mother, from Lord Mahon's house in Harley Street, describing the solemnity in detail.

One of his first duties, after the funeral, was to vindicate his father's memory from an accusation brought against him by Sir James Wright, a friend of Lord Bute, to the effect that he had at one time desired to form a political union with that Tory statesman. [2]

Early in 1779, not long after his father's death, he purchased, by his mother's help,

----

[1] *Quarterly Review*, vol. iv. p. 209.

[2] The details of this vindication are given in the Annual Register for 1778, pp. 244–264.

a set of chambers in the (then) New buildings of Lincoln's Inn. These he made for a short time his headquarters when in London, though he still kept on his rooms at Cambridge. The cost was about £1100, a sum which he calls "frightful" in a letter to his mother at the time ; he bought them with the view of attending Westminster Hall during the ensuing term, and also of being almost within "earshot" of the debates in St. Stephen's. In one of these visits to the House it is said that he was introduced on the steps of the throne to Fox, who was ten years his senior, and already in full enjoyment of his fame as an orator. As the discussion proceeded, Pitt repeatedly turned to him and said, "But surely, Mr. Fox, that might be met thus," or "Yes, but he lays himself open to the retort." Fox used to say that, although he had forgotten the exact subject under discussion on that night, he was much struck by the young man's precocity, who seemed to be "thinking only how all the speeches on both sides could be answered." Until these chambers could be got ready for him, he resided at Nerot's Hotel, in King Street, St. James' Square. [1]

During the brief interval which occurred between his college life and his entry into Parliament, Mr. Pitt seems to have passed a pleasant life, mixing in the best of West-End society, and especially in that of West-End clubs, and spending his Saturdays and Sundays often with his friend Wilberforce at his villa at Wimbledon. In spite of his gravity in mixed company, here he freely unbent himself, and indulged in all sorts of jokes and pranks and harmless fun. Among other games he was fond of fencing, or "foining"; and "one morning," writes Wilberforce, "we found the fruits of his early rising in the careful sowing of the garden-beds with the fragments of a dress-hat, in which Ryder [2] had overnight come down for the opera." So fond did he grow of Wilberforce, whom he had known slightly at Cambridge, that he

---

[1] Stanhope's "Life of Pitt," vol. i. p. 22.

[2] Mr. Nathaniel Ryder, then M.P. for Tiverton, afterwards created Lord Harrowby, and for some years a member of Mr. Pitt's Cabinet.

would sometimes spend a week or two with him, finding it a healthful luxury to sleep in country air, and to enjoy fresh-gathered peas and strawberries. He also made frequent short visits to Brighton, then called Brighthelmstone.

Pitt was an habitual frequenter of Goose-tree's Club, supping there almost every night during the winter of 1780-81. Though less formed for general popularity than his rival Fox, Pitt, when free from shyness and amongst intimate companions, was the very soul of conversation, and even of merriment. "He was," writes Wilber-force, "the wittiest man I ever knew, and, what was quite peculiar to himself, had at all times his wit under entire control. Others appeared struck by the unwonted association of brilliant images ; but every possible combination of ideas seemed always present to his mind, and he could at once produce whatever he desired." Wilberforce adds that he spent an evening in his company, "in memory of Shake-speare," at the Boar's Head in East Cheap, when Pitt was the most amusing of the party, though many professed wits were present, and the readiest and most apt in the required allusions. He entered into all the recognised amusements of young men of good birth and fair means, and displayed intense earnestness as often as he joined in games of chance; but these games he suddenly abandoned for ever, as soon as he perceived the danger of their fascinations.

It has been stated that Mr. Pitt was so fond of play that he "kept the bank" for the players at Goosetree's Club; but this, as Lord Stanhope and Mr. Wilberforce show, if it was ever true at all, was true of only a single night. That he was an habitual gambler, or that he approved of high play, is a libel on his character.

Another of his earliest and fastest friends was Henry Addington, afterwards Lord Sidmouth, but who will be mentioned throughout these pages by his former name. We learn incidentally from Wilberforce[1] that although Pitt and Adding-

---

[1] "Life," by his Sons, vol. iii. p. 211.

ton "had been friends from their childhood, like their fathers before them," but very few details of that early friendship are to be found. It appears probable that the two future Premiers met for the first time in 1772, when Dr. Addington took his family to Hayes, to see the children of Lord Chatham act a play written by themselves, as recorded in the previous chapter. They met, however, again in London, that common arena for all workers and toilers, when Pitt was waiting for parliamentary honours, and Addington was seeking for legal distinction ; but the first actual evidence of their acquaintance is to be found in a note from Pitt, appointing a meeting with him in December, 1782, at his brother's residence in Berkeley Square. From this time forward they became fast friends, and their careers ran parallel to each other almost to the end of Pitt's life. With Henry Dundas, afterwards Lord Melville, his acquaintance, or at all events his friendship, did not begin till after his entrance into St. Stephen's.

Another of his early friends was Lord

Mahon, afterwards Earl Stanhope, who as far back as 1772 had married his sister, Lady Hester Pitt. He had been educated at Geneva, where he had imbibed an ardent zeal for liberty and for science. Between him and William Pitt there now grew up a warm feeling of friendship; and, under Lord Chatham's guidance, the two young men looked forward to the same course in politics. But they were afterwards separated by Lord Mahon's strong enthusiasm in the cause of the French revolutionary party.

CHAPTER IV.

*Pitt enters Parliament—His Maiden Speech—
He "gains the Ear of the House"—His
Eloquence — Testimony of Sir N. W.
Wraxall, of, Lord North, and of Bishop
Goodenough.*

SCARCELY was William Pitt of full age,
when he took his seat in St. Stephen's.
The story of the way in which he entered
Parliament we learn from that amusing
gossiper, Sir Nathaniel W. Wraxall. Sir
James Lowther, a wealthy north-country
baronet, had no less than eight seats at his
command, for "pocket boroughs" had not
then been abolished; and it so happened
that the merits of the young man fresh
from Cambridge had reached the ears of
his father's old friend, the Duke of Rutland, who was intimate with the Lowthers.

Accordingly the Duke applied to Sir James, asking him at the General Election of 1780 to reserve one of his seats for his young friend. The seats, however, had all been bespoke ; but a few weeks later, in January, 1781, a chance vacancy occurring at Appleby, Mr. Pitt was returned by favour of its patron, without making any canvass or issuing an address, or even visiting the place. The constituency of Appleby at that time was Sir James Lowther himself, and his will was law ; and, for all that the borough records show, Mr. Pitt never set his eyes on the town which served as his stepping-stone to parliamentary life, and which he represented for nearly four years. During this and part of the following year, Pitt continued to occupy his chambers in Lincoln's Inn.

Having taken his seat, he remained silent for about five weeks before he made his maiden speech. He had already eaten his legal dinners, and been called to the Bar at Lincoln's Inn ; and it is said that in the previous spring he had gone the western circuit, and even " pocketed a fee."

But he was cut out for a higher destiny than "pocketing" guineas or defending criminals, and he knew and felt this to be the case. His motto from the first was *summa pete ;* and doubtless even from youth he meditated a career more short, more rapid, and more brilliant than " going circuit."   He was not ignorant of the powers which nature had planted in him, and which his father had cultivated with such care. Though the measure which he advocated was rejected by a large and decisive majority, yet his speech drew forth many compliments from old and experienced members,and established him in the goodwill and favour of the House, whose ear he had fairly gained.

Pitt entered Parliament within a few days of Richard Brinsley Sheridan, and, like him, he made his first essay in the House of Commons on the side of the Opposition, and as a member of that small party of which Lord Shelburne was the leader.   The occasion was the second reading of a Bill brought forward by Edmund Burke for the Reform of the

King's Household, and his speech was in reply to one delivered by Lord Nugent.

Mr. Pitt's first speech was remarkable not only for its eloquence, but for its plain-spoken honesty and its genuine "liberality." He said that "the Bill for the better regulation of His Majesty's civil list, and for abolishing several useless, expensive, and inconvenient places, would have come with more grace, and with more benefit to the public service, if it had sprung from the royal breast. His Majesty's ministers ought to have come forward and proposed a reduction in the civil list, to give the people the consolation of knowing that their sovereign participated in the sufferings of the empire, and presented an honourable example of retrenchment in the hour of general difficulty. . . . But if the members failed to do this . . . was that a reason why the House of Commons, His Majesty's public counsellors, should desist from a measure so congenial to the paternal feelings of the sovereign, so applicable to the wants and miseries of the people? . . . The abridgment of useless and unnecessary expense could be no abatement of royalty." He had the mortification, however, of seeing this very modest and moderate proposal rejected by a majority of 233 to 190 votes.

We have fortunately a brief record of this speech and its effect on the audience from the pen of Sir Nathaniel William Wraxall[1]:—

"The same composure, self-possession, and imposing dignity of manner which afterwards so eminently characterized him when seated on the Treasury Bench, distinguished Pitt in this first essay of his powers, though he still wanted three months of completing his twenty-second year. The same nervous, correct, and polished diction, free from any inaccuracy of language or embarrassment of deportment, which he subsequently displayed as Prime Minister, was equally manifested on this occasion. Formed for a popular assembly, he seemed made to guide its

---

[1] " Memoirs of my own Time," vol. i. pp. 62-64.

deliberations from the first moment that he addressed the members composing it. . . . All men beheld in him a future minister; and the Opposition, overjoyed at such an accession of strength, vied with each other in their encomiums, as well as in their predictions of his certain elevation."

Lord North, who was, or ought to have been, a good judge of such performances, used to say that Pitt's was the best first speech that he had ever heard; even the cynical Horace Walpole writes to his friend Sir Horace Mann, then abroad: "The two names of most *éclat* in the Opposition are names to which these walls have been much accustomed at the same period—Charles Fox and William Pitt, second son of Lord Chatham. Eloquence is the only one of our brilliant qualities that does not seem to have degenerated rapidly." William Wilberforce, too, tells a Yorkshire friend that, as the papers will have informed him, the younger Pitt comes out, as his father did before him, a ready-made orator, and adds in prophetic words,

"I doubt not but that I shall one day or other see him the first man in the country."

Wraxall adds the following particulars: "Great expectations having been formed of Pitt, a sort of anxious impatience for his coming forward possessed the assembly, which was strongly impressed, from a common report, with a belief of his hereditary talents and eloquence. He unquestionably commenced under most auspicious circumstances; his birth and his name, by resuscitating as it were the first Earl of Chatham, whose memory awakened such animating recollections, preparing every ear to be attentive, and thus removing all the impediments that present themselves in the way of ordinary men when attempting to address Parliament. But, sanguine as might be the opinions entertained of his ability, he far exceeded them, thus seeming to attain at his outset that object which other candidates for public fame or favour slowly and laboriously effect by length of time and regular gradations."

This likeness between the father and the son would seem to have struck other contemporaries of the latter most forcibly. At all events, Dr. Goodenough, afterwards Bishop of Carlisle, writes thus to Mr. Wilson, Pitt's early tutor, under date February 27th, 1781 : "I cannot resist the natural impulse of giving pleasure by telling you that the famous William Pitt, who made so capital a figure in the last reign, is happily restored to this country. He made his first public reappearance in the senate last night. All the old members recognised him instantly, and most of the young ones said he appeared the very man they had so often heard described. The language, the manner, the gesture, the action, were the same ; and there wanted only a few wrinkles in the face, and some marks of age, to identify the absolute person of the late Earl of Chatham."

This, however, it is only fair to state here, was not the verdict of all the London world at that time. Lord Stanhope, for example, remarks that carefully as he had been trained by his father, "their styles of oratory and their direction of knowledge were not only different, but almost, it may be said, opposite. Lord Chatham excelled in fiery bursts of eloquence, Pitt in a luminous array of arguments. On no point was Pitt so strong as on finance; on none was Chatham so weak."

In discussing the question of heredity, it has often been said that few great men have handed on their great qualities to their children; but it must be admitted that the two William Pitts, father and son, form a strong exception to any such rule; and it is for this reason that I have dwelt at greater length than I should otherwise have done upon the family pedigree and Mr. Pitt's early traits of character.

How speedily the anticipations of Pitt's friends and contemporaries were realized will be shown in the succeeding chapters.

CHAPTER V.

*Pitt's Second and Third Speeches—He goes Cir-
cuit—His Speeches on the American Colonies,
and on the Defeat of Lord Cornwallis in
North America—The Ministry of Lord
North : its Fall—Lord Rockingham succeeds
as Premier.*

ON the 31st of May Mr. Pitt made his
second speech in the House; it was on the
subject of a Bill to continue an Act of the
previous Session for the appointment of
Commissioners of the Public Accounts.
The subject was one which suited his taste
for financial matters ; and the gist of the
speech was that, as the nation had entrusted
the House of Commons with the control
of the national expenditure, it would not
be right to delegate any part of that power
and responsibility to persons who were not
members of that body. He, however, failed
to convince the House, and Lord North

carried the negative by a majority of more than two to one.

He spoke again on June 12th, on a far more important subject, and one more worthy of his powers; namely, the motion of Mr. Fox in favour of making peace with the Transatlantic colonies. Here again, however, Lord North, supported by the King's secret influence, carried the day, the votes being 172 to 99 against going into committee on the question. In the course of this speech Pitt eloquently vindicated his father's memory from the charge of having supported that war. His father, he said, had "most heartily reprobated the American War in all its parts, as well with respect to the principle on which it was taken up as to its progress and the ultimate objects to which it pointed." With respect to himself, "in whatever point of view he considered the war, he was the more confirmed in the opinions that he had early formed concerning its origin and tendency. It was conceived in injustice; it was brought forth and nurtured in folly; its footsteps were marked with blood,

persecution, and devastation. It was pro-
ductive of misery of every kind. The mischief, however, recoiled on this unhappy
country, which was by it drained of its
vital resources both of men and of trea-
sure."

Parliament being prorogued on the 18th
of July, Mr. Pitt again went circuit, and
was engaged at Salisbury as a junior in a
bribery case arising out of an election at
Cricklade, and later in an action for criminal conversation at Exeter. The circuit
ended, he visited his mother at Burton
Pynsent, and then returned to his chambers
in London.

When Parliament met again in November, the King's speech announced the news
of the surrender of Lord Cornwallis at
York Town, which caused great depression
to the Ministry and proportionately increased the hopes of the Opposition. Fox
moved an amendment on the address, and
he was supported by both Edmund Burke
and by Pitt, who was loudly applauded.
A fortnight later (December, 1781) Pitt
again spoke on the Army Estimates, when,

according to Horace Walpole, he displayed "amazing logical abilities, exceed-
ing all he had hitherto shown, and making
men doubt whether he would not prove
superior even to Charles Fox." His
speech was in support of the usual address
to the King, and in reply to sundry comments passed on it by Burke in an almost
ludicrous manner.

During the delivery of this speech he
suffered some slight interruption from
Lord George Germaine and Mr. Welbore
Ellis, who were whispering aloud. On
this Mr. Pitt paused for a moment, and
then said quietly, in a tone of reproof, " I
will wait till the Agamemnon of the present day has finished his consultation with
the Nestor of the Treasury Bench." The
effect of this happy classical allusion was
electrical, and he suffered no further interruption. Burke exclaimed that he was
"not merely a chip of the old block, but
the old block itself"; and Charles James
Fox was so delighted with him that he
carried him off to Brooks's Club, where
he proposed him for immediate election as

a member.   It may be as well to add here,
though somewhat in anticipation of the
actual order of events, that Mr. Pitt remained a member of Brooks's for several
years, though he never frequented it as
Fox did, and rarely appeared within its
doors after he took office under the Crown.

In the early part of the following year
(1782) these attacks on Lord North and
his policy were renewed from time to time,
and Mr. Pitt spoke frequently in support
of them.   The minister, however, was still
in a majority, though a decreasing one;
and therefore the public surprise was not
great when it was announced, on the 20th
of March, that Lord North had resigned—
an event which Pitt's speeches had helped
more or less directly to bring about.   He
was succeeded in April by Lord Rockingham, who it was hoped would be able to
rally round him all or most of the moderate
men on either side of the House.   But his
possession of Downing Street lasted for
little more than three months, and his
death in the following July again broke up
parties and threw the Administration into
confusion.

CHAPTER VI.

Mr. Pitt brings forward his Motion for Parliamentary Reform — Supports Bills for shortening Parliaments, and for preventing Bribery at Elections—Dr. Gifford's Vindication of Pitt's Conduct.

IN the following May, while Lord Rockingham was at the head of the Treasury, Mr. Pitt, true to his genuinely progressive instincts, brought forward his promised resolutions in favour of "a Reform in the Parliamentary Representation of the Country." He avowed that dissatisfaction at the existing representation had been largely caused by the misfortunes and disasters of the last few years, which had led the people to look and see if there were not something radically wrong at home. Hence had sprung up a variety of schemes founded on visionary and im-

 E

practicable ideas of reform. "It was not for him," he said, "with unhallowed hands to touch the venerable pile of the Constitution, and deface the fabric—it was sufficiently sad to see it stand in need of repair ; but the more he revered it, and the more he wished to secure its duration to the latest posterity, the greater he felt the necessity of guarding against its decay."

There were, he said, three expedients: the first was the extension of the suffrage to every citizen ; the second was to abolish all "rotten boroughs" ; and the third to add to the representation of the counties and of the metropolis. The first plea he "utterly rejected and condemned"; the second also he could not approve, on the somewhat sentimental ground that they were "deformities which in some degree disfigured the fabric of the Constitution, but which could not be removed without endangering the whole pile"; but the third satisfied his idea of the wants of the country. Accordingly he moved the following resolutions :—

1. " That it is the opinion of this House that measures are highly necessary to be taken for the future prevention of bribery and expense at elections."

2. " That for the future, when the majority of voters for any borough shall be convicted of gross and notorious corruption before a Select Committee of that House appointed to try the merits of any election, such borough shall be disfranchised, and the minority of voters not so convicted shall be entitled to vote for the county in which such borough shall be situated."

3. " That an addition of knights of the shire [1] and of representatives of the metropolis shall be made to the state of the representation."

These resolutions were negatived, though by a majority of only twenty votes (141 to 161). Pitt writes to his mother quite contentedly on May 15th: " My defeat on parliamentary reform was much more

[1] It had been suggested by Lord Chatham several years previously that an addition of 100 should be made to the county members.

complete than I expected; still, if the question was to be lost, the discussion has not been without its use."

Two days later Mr. Pitt supported Alderman Sawbridge's motion in favour of shortening the duration of parliaments, and spoke in its favour; and in June we find him advocating a Bill introduced by his relative and friend, Lord Mahon, for preventing bribery at elections.

But, though Pitt was at this time a decided reformer, he was not an advocate of any chimerical or utopian measures. His plan of parliamentary reform must be admitted to have contained nothing hostile to the spirit and principles of the British Constitution; it included nothing which could cause the most timid of the Tory party one moment of dread or apprehension. The majority of the House of Commons, however, based their objections to it on the grounds that the nation did not really desire the proposed innovation; that the growing and prosperous towns had not asked for the franchise; and that the representatives of rotten boroughs had frequently a large stake in the country, and were therefore intimately concerned in its welfare. It was further urged that it would be unwise to change the present system of representation, which fully secured the rights and privileges of the people, for the uncertain prospects held forward by Mr. Pitt. In Dr. Paley's opinion, no new plan of representation would be likely to " collect together more wisdom or produce firmer integrity " than that which resulted from the Constitution as it then stood ; but it will be seen from the following extract that Gifford—the Tory biographer of Pitt—differs widely from the Doctor on this subject :—

" Mr. Pitt's new scheme certainly *did* tend to collect together more wisdom, and to produce a greater proportion of firm integrity. And, without being influenced by any architectural notions of order and proportion, which, applied to a system of representation, would be perfectly ridiculous, it may safely be contended that no solid or justifiable inference can be drawn from known effects in favour of those decayed boroughs, which appear, not merely to superficial or hasty observers, but to men of sense and reflection, most exceptionable and absurd. It would, indeed, be insanity to subvert long-established institutions, in order to introduce any vague and indefinite plan of reform ; but subversion, it must be repeated, is not necessary for the purpose of improvement ; whatever exists that is conformable with the fundamental principles of the system may remain ; but excrescences, which time and fortuitous circumstances have produced, may be gradually removed, until they shall be totally eradicated ; and the system, far from being injured by such an operation, will be meliorated, strengthened, and confirmed. It is not improbable, however, that Mr. Pitt, at a more advanced period of his political life, adopted the opinions of Dr. Paley, since, as has been observed before, his sentiments on the subject of parliamentary reform underwent a material change. But, though it cannot be supposed that such a change took place but after the most mature consideration, and on grounds that were perfectly satisfactory to Mr. Pitt, still his arguments retain their original force; they must be tried by their own merits; and, it is apprehended that whoever examines them with an attentive and impartial mind, will be led to acknowledge their validity." [1]

This surely is a very high testimony to Pitt's wisdom, considering the quarter from which it comes. On this question, at all events, how wide and how permanent was Pitt's influence upon the nation is shown by the fact that Lord John Russell and the other Whig leaders, who agitated for reform during the regency and reign of George IV., and who carried it under William IV., based their strongest arguments in addressing the Tory House of Commons on the ground that their Reform Bill was identical in principle with the measure first proposed by Pitt in 1783. On this part of Mr. Pitt's career, the following extract from "Gladstone and His

[1] Gifford's "Life of Pitt," vol. i. p. 131.

Cotemporaries" may not be out of place :—

"Fifty years earlier (than the Regency of George IV.) the great Earl of Chatham had advocated a scheme of Parliamentary Reform which he did not live to bring before the Government ; and the attempt had been renewed by his illustrious son, William Pitt, in 1782, and again in 1785, but without success. The French Revolution had the effect of changing Pitt himself into an enemy of the opinions which he formerly advocated. . . . On the other hand, petitions signed by thousands of persons were presented to Parliament from the large towns—from Sheffield, from Birmingham, and from Edinburgh—the latter containing so many names that it extended over the whole length of the floor of the House. Among these petitions the most important was one from the 'friends of the people,' presented by Mr. (afterwards Earl) Grey, which was so ably and temperately drawn that it may be said to have been the true precursor of most of the remonstrances in the cause of Parliamentary Reform which have since been recognised. In it the petitioners offered to prove that upwards of ninety-seven members were actually nominated, and seventy more indirectly appointed by Peers and the Treasury, and that ninety-one Commoners procured the election of 139 more, so that 306 members, at that time an absolute majority of the House of Commons, were returned by 160 persons. 'I assert,' said Mr. Grey, 'that this is the condition of England. If you say it is *not* so, do justice by calling on us for the proof; but if it be the condition of England, shall it not be redressed?'"[1]

[1] "Gladstone and His Cotemporaries," vol. i. pp. 1, 2.

CHAPTER VII.

Recognition of American Independence—Break up of Parties in England—Lord Rockingham succeeded by Lord Shelburne—Pitt becomes Chancellor of the Exchequer—Resigns with Lord Shelburne.

THE conclusion of peace with North America, and the formal recognition of the United States as an independent nation, gave rise, as might be expected, not only to fierce discussions in the British Parliament, but also to a general break up of parties. This was the fault in a great measure of the obstinacy of King George, who chose to "rule" as well as to "reign," even at the cost of losing our Transatlantic colonies. It also involved a succession of short-lived Administrations, which threw political affairs at home into a hopeless chaos, as we have seen, first by the resignation of Lord North, and then by the sudden death of Lord Rockingham. At this latter juncture (July, 1782), undoubtedly Charles James Fox was the proper person to have been called on now to direct the counsels of the nation ; but the King " would have none of him," and chose Lord Shelburne instead ; and, after a fruitless attempt on the part of Fox's friends to get the Premiership for the Duke of Portland, the latter withdrew in a body and passed into Opposition, while Pitt elected to stand by Lord Shelburne (whom the King had named as Premier), giving him an independent support, but at first declining to join his Ministry. On the retirement of Fox and the Duke of Portland, however, a few weeks later, Lord Shelburne reinforced his Cabinet by the admission of Earl Temple, one of the King's most intimate friends ; room was also found for Mr. Thomas Townshend, as a Secretaryship of State, and for Mr. Pitt, as Chancellor of the Exchequer.

Pitt had already given out to his friends

that if any post in the Ministry should be offered to him, he would not accept it "without a seat in the Cabinet." But he held that office for only a very few months, not long enough, certainly, to give him an opportunity of showing to the country that ability in matters of finance with which he was even then credited, in spite of his youth, and for which he was afterwards so. remarkable. How high an estimate was formed of Pitt's value at this early period in life is shown by the following extract from a letter written by Sir Gilbert Elliot, afterwards Lord Minto, in July, 1782: "The present Government (Lord Shelburne's) is gaining strength wherever it can, and has made a valuable acquisition in William Pitt, to whom, at the age of two or three and twenty, Lord Shelburne has offered either the Chancellorship of the Exchequer, or the Secretaryship of State, as he pleases."

It was necessary, however, to the Government, if it was to be permanent, to secure support in every direction; for, strong as it might be, it had to reckon with a still stronger Opposition, made up of the supporters of Fox and the adherents of Lord North, for though he had ceased to hold office, the latter had a following. Either the one section or the other, it was clear, must be gained over if Lord Shelburne's Administration was to stand. Lord Shelburne himself inclined to make overtures to Lord North, while Pitt inclined to the opposite side. In the end Pitt prevailed, and offers were made by them jointly to Fox, who consented. Still the efforts to form a stable Ministry were fruitless, owing to the personal jealousies of individuals who were not willing to sacrifice them to the public good.

In February, 1783, a motion was made in the House of Commons, really against Lord Shelburne, though in form it was a vote of censure on the peace lately made with France and Spain, and on the provisional treaty with America. It was on this occasion that Pitt, having to defend these measures in the Commons, and stung to the quick by the factious hostility of two sections of the Opposition who were united in little else than the wish to embarrass Lord Shelburne and drive him from office, uttered the memorable and oft-quoted words :—

"I repeat, sir, that it is not this treaty, but the Earl of Shelburne alone, whom the movers of this question are desirous to wound. This is the object that has raised this storm of faction ; this is the aim of the unnatural coalition to which I have alluded. If, however, the baneful alliance is not already formed, if this ill-omened marriage is not already solemnized, I know a just and lawful impediment, and in the name of the public safety I forbid the banns."

The other passage rose to a still higher pitch of eloquence :—

"Unused as I am to the factious and jarring clamours of this day's debate, I look up to the independent part of the House, and to the public at large, if not for that impartial approbation which my conduct deserves, at least for that acquittal from blame to which my innocence entitles me. . . . I am, notwithstanding, at the disposal of this House, and with their decision, whatever it may be, I will cheerfully comply. It is impossible to deprive me of those feelings which must always result from the sincerity of my best endeavours to fulfil with integrity every official engagement. You may take from me, sir, the privileges and emoluments of place ; but you cannot, and you shall not, take from me those habitual and warm regards for the prosperity of Great Britain which constitute the honour, the happiness, and the pride of my life, and which I trust death alone can extingush. And with this consolation, I hope I shall soon be able to forget the loss of power and the loss of fortune, though I affect not to despise them.

> "Laudo manentem : si celeres quatit
>   Pennas, resigno quæ dedit. . . .
>   . . . . probamque
>   Pauperiem sine dote quæro."

The fact of his omission of the words which should fill up the *lacuna* in the above lines was duly appreciated as a proof of the young statesman's modesty, and drew down the cheers of the House, whose members at that time were perhaps better acquainted with the works of Horace and other Latin poets than they are now-a-days, and quoted them with greater freedom and frequency.

In the event Lord Shelburne resigned, finding it impossible to carry on the Government against the combined factions, and Mr. Pitt gave notice to his friends that he held his official post only till his successor was appointed.

In laying down his office, however, Lord Shelburne did not advise the King to bestow it upon any of the chiefs of the new coalition, but pressed upon His Majesty an idea which Dundas and other friends had pressed upon himself, to make Mr. Pitt Prime Minister. The Chancellor concurred in the advice, and the King, eager to escape the yoke already fitted to his neck—the yoke of the great Whig houses—grasped at the suggestion. He sent at once to Mr. Pitt, offering him the headship of the Treasury, with full authority to nominate his colleagues.

At first Mr. Pitt was inclined to accept

the onerous duty placed upon him by the King ; but after consulting with his friends he declined it, though much pressed by his sovereign to undertake it. " Thus," remarks Lord Stanhope, "was the whole power of the State, without stint or reservation, laid at the feet of a younger son of a far from wealthy family, of a junior barrister who had received but very few briefs, of a stripling who had not quite attained the age of twenty-four. It is perhaps the most glorious tribute to early promise that any history records." [1]

[1] Stanhope's " Life of Pitt," vol. i. p. 82.

F

CHAPTER VIII.

The Duke of Portland and his "Coalition" Ministry—Pitt in Opposition—He Opposes Fox's India Bill—Defeat of the Coalition Ministry—Pitt makes a Tour to France.

DURING the whole month of March, 1783, there was a ministerial *interregnum;* but on the 2nd of April was formed the so-called "Coalition" Ministry, so famed in history. Mr. Pitt having declined the post, the Duke of Portland was appointed First Lord of the Treasury; Lord North became Secretary of State for the Home Department, and Mr. Fox for Foreign Affairs; Lord John Cavendish was made Chancellor of the Exchequer; Lord Keppel took the Admiralty, Lord Stormont the Presidency of the Council, Lord Carlisle the Privy Seal; Edmund Burke was made Paymaster-General; Mr. Charles Townshend, Master-

General of the Ordnance; and Mr. Fitz-Patrick, Secretary at War.

The above list includes the names of several persons who had previously stood in a more or less hostile attitude to each other; and the nation at large, which, much as it loves judicious compromises, does not love "coalitions," regarded the new Ministry with mistrust. Nor was it long before the House of Commons, if it could be said then to represent public opinion, refused its support to the Cabinet, and wrought its fall. On the 18th of April Mr. Fox brought forward "a Bill for vesting the affairs of the East India Company in the hands of certain Commissioners for the benefit of the proprietors and the public, and for the better government of the territorial possessions and dependencies in India." The introduction of this Bill excited the most violent opposition. The bold and comprehensive ideas displayed in it caused a profound sensation both in and out of Parliament, whilst its innovations and its extraordinary delegations of power created an intense feeling of repugnance. The chief objections urged in detail against it were its arbitrary invasion of the chartered rights of the East India Company, and the dangerous authority and unlimited patronage which it lodged in the hands of the new directorship that it contemplated.

It was on this occasion that Pitt first came prominently forward as leader of the Opposition to the ministers, principally on the ground that the charter of the Company ought not to be set aside without absolute necessity, and that the Bill was an infraction of the Constitution itself; for that, by throwing the whole patronage of India into the hands of the Commissioners, it tended to create a fourth estate in the realm incompatible with the nature of the Government and independent of the Crown—a power which might prove most destructive to the other branches of the legislature.

The controversy about the charter of the East India Company was taken up vigorously out of doors, and a flood of literature, serious and satirical, was the immediate result. The metropolis was deluged with pamphlets intended to make the Bill odious to the nation, and both the Company and the City of London presented strong petitions to Parliament against it. The strength of the Coalition Ministry was shown by the fact that the Bill at first was passed by a majority of two to one; but Earl Temple used his private and "backstairs" influence with the King, persuading him that the Bill, if carried into law, would fetter and cripple the power of the Crown. The King then addressed to Lord Temple a letter in which he said that he "should deem those who voted for the Bill, not only not his friends, but his enemies." The consequence was that when the Bill came to the Upper House the ministers were left in a minority, and the Bill was lost. On the same day a messenger brought to the two Secretaries of State an order from the King to deliver up their seals of office forthwith, and on the following day the rest of the Cabinet were dismissed.

At the close of the session Mr. Pitt took a short holiday on the Continent. In his youth he had never made "the grand tour," and the French language had not formed part of his early education. His companions were Mr. Wilberforce and Mr. Eliot. He went by Calais first to Rheims, and thence to Paris. He was presented by our Ambassador, the Duke of Manchester, to Louis XVI. and Marie Antoinette at Fontainebleau. "His name," writes Sir N. W. Wraxall, "and the fame of his distinguished abilities, which had preceded him, disposed all to admire him; but the King, in compliance with that stupid etiquette which interdicted him from speaking to foreigners when presented at Court, added to his natural shyness, did not, I believe, exchange one word with Pitt. The Queen, whose superior energy of mind emancipated her from such restraints, treated him with the utmost distinction, and entered into conversation with him, as far as his cold manner, increased by his imperfect knowledge of the French language, would permit her to engage him in discourse. 'Monsieur,' said she to him on his retiring, with a manner even more expressive than the words, '*Je suis charmée de vous voir et de vous avoir vue.*'"

Some further details have been preserved of this, the only visit to the Continent which Pitt ever made. Nearly all are derived from the letters and the published Diary of Mr. Wilberforce. At Rheims, Pitt had many conversations with Abbé de Lageard, a highly intelligent gentleman, then the Archbishop's delegate, and afterwards an emigrant in England. One day, Lord Stanhope tells us, as the orator was expressing in warm terms his admiration of the political system which prevailed at home, the Abbé asked him, since all human things were perishable, in what part the British Constitution might first be expected to decay? Pitt mused for a moment, and then answered, "The part of our Constitution that will first perish is the prerogative of the King and the authority of the House of Peers."

"I am much surprised," said the Abbé, "that a country so moral as England can submit to be governed by such a spendthrift and such a rake as Fox; it seems to show that you are less moral than you claim to be."

"The remark is just," Pitt replied, "but you have not been under the wand of the magician."

On French institutions also they sometimes conversed. Pitt made many careful inquiries, and summed up his impressions in the following words : " Sir, you have no political liberty ; but as to civil liberty, you have more of it than you suppose."

"It is remarkable," writes Lord Stanhope, " that this is the very conclusion which, in treating of that period seventy years afterwards, the work of De Tocqueville has with so much force of argument maintained."

A silly story, for which Horace Walpole is responsible, makes out that during this tour there was some proposal of a marriage between Mr. Pitt and the daughter of M. Neckar, the French financier and statesman, but that Pitt negatived the idea, declaring that he was " already married to his country "! Lord Stanhope rejects the story as apocryphal, and the answer is too theatrical to accord with Pitt's taste and mode of expression.

CHAPTER IX.

THE Premiership was now again offered by the King to Mr. Pitt, who, though little more than twenty-four years of age, and necessarily with a very brief experience of political work, bravely took in his hands the helm of the State. He became both First Lord of the Treasury and Chancellor of the Exchequer, his colleagues being Lord Gower as President of the Council, Lord Sydney as Secretary of State for the Home Department, and Lord Carmarthen for Foreign Affairs; while, Lord Thurlow was Lord Chancellor, Lord Howe First Lord of the Admiralty, the Duke of Richmond Master-General of the Ordnance, Lord Mulgrave and Mr. W. W. Grenville Joint Paymasters-General, Mr. Henry Dundas (afterwards Lord Melville) becoming at the same time Treasurer of the Navy.

Thus, in December, 1783, Mr. Pitt, the "boy" of twenty-four, became on his own terms Prime Minister, the celebrated Mrs. Crewe and other friends of Fox declaring that "after all it would be only a mince-pie Administration." It is remarkable that in his Cabinet of seven, only one, Mr. Pitt himself, was a member of the House of Commons.

When he was summoned thus by the King to occupy the highest position in His Majesty's councils, Pitt was surrounded by difficulties of the most formidable character, the greatest, perhaps, that any Prime Minister of England ever had to grapple with. He had to contend against a majority of the Commons, including men well versed in all the schemes and manœuvres of parliamentary warfare, amongst whom were Edmund Burke, Richard Brinsley Sheridan, Charles James Fox, and Lord North. The relations of England with foreign countries and the now independent colonies in North America, required the most careful treatment and the greatest vigilance. Our finances at the close of an unsuccessful war were also in great disorder. The East India question had especially become of pressing importance ; and it was necessary that all Pitt's energies should be directed to the task of framing a new measure to take the place of that proposed by Fox, but which the House of Lords had declined to accept. By the greatest exertions on the part of Mr. Pitt and his colleagues, a draft Bill was prepared, and, best of all, approved by the Court of Directors and the proprietors of the East India Company, in time to be submitted to the House in the following January.

A variety of motions, all more or less hostile, were brought forward and carried against Mr. Pitt on the very first day in which he appeared in the House as First Lord of the Treasury ; but undismayed, and strong in the knowledge that he enjoyed the King's confidence, he calmly and coolly gave notice that next day he should move for leave to bring in his India Bill.

"So far," he said, "from violating its chartered rights, he had sought to frame his measure in amicable concert with the Company, while at the same time he trusted that it would prove most effectual for the reformation of abuses. He proposed to establish a new department of the State, without, however, any new salaries—a Board of Control, which should divide with the directors the entire administration of India, but leave the patronage untouched. It is my idea," he added, "that this shall really be a Board of political control, and not, as the former was, a Board of political influence."

No sooner had he sat down than Fox, without allowing a moment of consideration to his rival's scheme, started up and denounced every part of it, though in principle it did not differ very widely from his own measure of the previous year. In spite of Fox's speech, an attempt was made by some of the more moderate members of the Opposition to bring about an agreement between Pitt and his rival ; but it failed. Mr. Pitt knew that his "strength was to sit still" and allow the waves from their ranks to break at his feet. Being questioned as to his intentions, he declined to state whether he would or would not advise the King to dissolve Parliament, and patiently awaited their further assaults. In the event, the Bill was thrown out by a considerable majority towards the end of January.

At this juncture occurred an event, trifling in itself, which proved of immense assistance to Pitt by establishing his character for unselfishness and indifference to those mercenary motives by which it is to be feared that most of his contemporaries, and perhaps some of his successors also, were too often influenced. A valuable sinecure of £3,000 a year, the Clerkship of the Pells, fell vacant, and both his friends and his foes expected that Mr. Pitt would secure it for himself, as indeed he had every right to do ; but he refused to touch it, though his own personal income, as a younger son, was very small. By disposing of it in another quarter, a saving was made to the country ; and he had the satisfaction of knowing that he had established for life a character for disinterestedness. "It is a great thing," writes Macaulay, "for a man who has only three hundred a year to be able to show that he considers three thousand a year as mere dirt beneath his feet when compared with the public interest and the public esteem."

But to return to parliamentary affairs. The nation began now to see that Fox had overshot his mark, and had entered into a struggle against the King—a contest, to use the words of Dr. Johnson, "whether the nation should be ruled by the sceptre of George the Third or by the tongue of Fox." False to the traditions of all English citizens, he had "seemed to question two of the most important and most undoubted of the royal prerogatives—the right to appoint his ministers and the right to dissolve Parliament. He refused to grant his rival any respite, and he treated him with such a marked want of courtesy that his violent conduct served as a counterpoise to the violent conduct of the King. Day after day, therefore, and week after week was the young minister urged to advise an immediate dissolution. But his sagacity led him to read the signs of the times more clearly than did his friends. He saw that Fox's popularity was on the wane, and that the longer he could postpone an appeal to the country the better would be his chances of success." Even the King pressed on him to dissolve, but he still remained firm ; nor did he yield until three weeks after Fox had carried an Address to the Crown for the dismissal of the Ministry, and he had gained what he thought an advantageous opportunity. On the 23rd of March the nation learned the news ; and in spite of the abstraction of the Great Seal of England from the Lord Chancellor's house, on the following day, a new seal was made, and the Parliament was dissolved.

The result of the election showed that the appeal to the country was not made in vain. No less than a hundred and fifty of his opponents lost their seats, and the new Premier was placed at the head of a corresponding majority. Those who lost their seats on this occasion were long known as " Fox's Martyrs." Mr. Pitt, who never was much attached to "rotten" boroughs, was glad to leave Appleby and to come in for the University of Cambridge, which he continued to represent until his death ; and among his other friends Mr. Wilberforce was elected for Yorkshire as well as for his old constituency at Hull. Fox, doubtful of being able to retain his seat for Westminster, was glad to accept a seat for the Kirkwall boroughs in the Orkneys from his friend, Sir Thomas Dundas. Pitt doubtless owed much of his victory to the disgust of the nation at the coalition which had been formed against him, and much also to the alarm caused by Fox's India Bill ; but it would be a mistake to suppose that his supporters were all Tories ; they were men who had hitherto been wide asunder, Dissenters as well as Churchmen, friends of the King, and advocates of popular rights—men as far apart as Jenkinson and John Wilkes. For, as Macaulay observes, " the coalition had at once alienated the most zealous Tories from North and the most zealous Whigs from Fox."

The election fixed Pitt in his seat even more firmly than he or his friends had expected, and, supported as he was by the personal favour of the King, he found himself each month at the head of a stronger party. He now began to bend all his efforts to the duties of his situation. Though more than a year had passed since the conclusion of peace with America, the constant strife of parties had prevented each successive First Lord of the Treasury from adopting any large and effectual measures to recover the country from the exhaustion to which it had been brought by a long and expensive war. Commerce was stagnant, the national credit was depressed, and the public funds, even after an interval of peace, at the lowest war prices. Added to this, the national income, unequal to its expenditure even if collected to the full, was diminished by large and systematic frauds, especially on the excise; and the affairs of India were in a state of unsatisfactory confusion. The first and most urgent matter before him, therefore, was finance. To check the smuggling of tea, he reduced the duty on it to a great extent, imposing instead an additional window tax. As to the East India Company, he proposed one Bill enabling its directors to divide eight per cent. interest on their capital, and another to give them some respite in the payment of sundry duties to the National Exchequer, and other financial advantages. These having been carried, he further proposed to extend considerably the powers of the Board of Control, even to the extent of allowing it to transmit orders to India without previously submitting them to the directors at home. Other clauses of the Bill had for their objects the prevention of unjust gains made by the Company's servants under the name of presents, and the establishment of a new tribunal for the punishment of East Indian delinquents. So high, however, did party feeling run, that most of these measures were strongly opposed by Fox, Burke, and Sheridan; but they did not meet with any large amount of success. In the only division which their opponents tried upon the general principle, they were defeated by 271 to 60 votes, and Pitt's Bill passed with equal ease through the House of Lords.

At this period of his life Pitt is described in not very attractive colours by Sir N. W. Wraxall.[1]

" In the formation of his person he was tall and slender, but without elegance or grace. In his manners he was repulsive; he was cold, stiff, and without suavity or amenity. He seemed never to invite approach, or to encourage acquaintance, though when addressed he could be polite and communicative, and occasionally even gracious. Smiles were not natural to him, even when seated on the Treasury Bench.

---

[1] " Memoirs of my own Time," vol. v. p. 633.

. . . From the instant that Pitt entered the door of the House of Commons, he advanced up the floor with a quick firm step, his head erect and thrown back, looking neither to the right nor the left, nor favouring with a nod or a glance any of the individuals seated on either side, among whom many who possessed £5,000 a year would have been gratified even by so slight a mark of attention. It was not thus that North or Fox treated Parliament."

But in spite of his haughty and supercilious manner, he had contrived to inspire his supporters in the House of Commons with almost absolute devotion and obedience. Thus we find Gibbon writing from Lausanne to Fox:—

" They are biassed by the splendour of young Pitt, and it is a fair and honourable prejudice. A youth of five-and-twenty, who raises himself to the government of an empire by the power of genius and the reputation of virtue, is a circumstance unparalleled in history, and, in a general view, is not less glorious to the country than to himself."

The fact is that Pitt had not merely secured his high position by the results of the General Election of 1784. He had done much more. He had tested the patience of the public by that most trying of all tests, the imposition of new taxes, and he had not found it wanting. He had settled also for many years to come the future principles of our government of India. "At this date, the autumn of 1784, he was," to use the words of Macaulay, in his "Essay on William Pitt," " the greatest subject that England had seen during many generations. His father had never been so powerful, nor had Walpole, nor Marlborough."

During this period, Pitt was living at Holwood, a country house which he had bought between Keston and Bromley in Kent, not far from his birthplace at Hayes, and here he was constantly visited by Addington, Wilberforce, Dundas, Eden, and others of his parliamentary friends. After a long and weary day's labour town he would return hither late at nigh in a post-chaise, often at considerable risk, as the roads were at that time far from safe. Thus, in 1786, when Addington and Lord Apsley, afterwards Earl Bathurst, were returning in a chaise to London, after dining with him at Holwood, they were stopped by foot-pads on the highway between Bromley and Lewisham, and robbed of their watches and purses.

Holwood continued to be Pitt's favourite home for nearly twenty years, until he sold it in 1802. It was while seated, along with the great statesman, under an oak in the grounds at Holwood that Wilberforce resolved, and communicated to Pitt his resolution, to bring forward in the House of Commons his motion for the abolition of the slave-trade. The venerable oak still stands; it is known as "Pitt's oak," "Wilberforce's oak," and "Emancipation oak;" and a stone seat placed by Lord Stanhope with a suitable inscription in 1862 marks the consecrated spot. It was visited by Wilberforce's son, the late Bishop Wilberforce, in 1862, and the visit is thus mentioned in the Bishop's diary:—

"Examined the Wilberforce oak. Saw

Mr. Pitt's old carter boy, now eighty-two and clear in his remembrance. Mr. Pitt, he said, took in from the farm the ground sloping below the oak; he planted all except the old oaks. He used to get the trees from Brompton: I used to go in a cart for them. He was very particular about the planting. He was a very nice sort of man, and would do what any one asked him in one way or another."

CHAPTER X.

WE must now pass back from the rural pleasures of Holwood to the House of Commons and the strife of parties. For many months Pitt had been closely studying the question of Reform, and he had spoken on the subject with Mr. Christopher Wyvill and others whose names were prominently connected with the cause. In answer to their requests, he again promised to bring forward a measure during the coming session, and to use his most strenuous efforts to carry it through Parliament. The state of the representation of the people in the House of Commons had given rise to so much discontent that, with the lapse of time, the matter of its reform had become really urgent. Members of Parliament were returned by corporations, freeholders, or burgage-tenants of numerous small towns, and the consequence was that peers and wealthy commoners had purchased property in the small boroughs in order that they might increase their political influence. These "boroughmongers," as a rule, bought up the freeholds or burgage-tenures in small constituencies, so that they might bring the number of voters completely under their own control. In many of these "nomination boroughs" seats were bought and sold, and corruption was everywhere rampant.

Although the King was very much disinclined to measures of Reform, Mr. Pitt succeeded in obtaining His Majesty's nominal and reluctant consent to the proposed measure, together with a declaration that the royal influence would not be used against it. Pitt at this time wrote to the

Duke of Rutland, expressing his conviction that Parliamentary Reform must, sooner or later, be carried in both countries ; " and," he added, "if it is well done, the sooner the better." The difficulties of his task, however, were enormous, and more especially was this the case within the walls of Parliament. The motion was brought before the House on the 18th of April. There was a crowded attendance of members, and of strangers in the gallery. The proposal of Mr. Pitt was to disfranchise thirty-six decayed boroughs, each returning two members, and to assign the seventy-two seats to the largest counties, and to the cities of London and Westminster. His scheme further included the admission of copyholders to the franchise on the same footing as freeholders, and the abolition of compulsory voting in the " rotten " boroughs. In order to compensate the borough proprietors, a fund of a million sterling was to be founded, and an invitation was to be sent to each borough to apply for a scheme of reform by petition from two-thirds of its electors. This was, perhaps, the most important feature in the Bill, and it bears a fairly close analogy to the means by which the Union with Ireland was afterwards carried. Mr. Pitt anticipated that this course of action would very shortly bring about the extinction of the thirty-six smallest boroughs. In the future, if any other boroughs should become decayed, and sink below a certain number of houses and inhabitants, power was to be given to them to surrender their franchise on an adequate consideration, when their privilege of returning members to Parliament would be transferred to thriving and populous towns.

In spite, however, of all his influence as Prime Minister—thanks partly to the opposition of Lord North—Mr. Pitt's most moderate and wise Bill for Parliamentary Reform was rejected by a majority of 248 to 174.

The rejection of the Bill was really due to the secret influence of His Majesty among his own personal "friends," who knew that the favour of the King was a surer road to promotion and reward than that of his minister, who might rule in Downing Street to-day, and be left on the cold benches of the Opposition to-morrow. But Pitt accepted the verdict contentedly and without repining, considering the result as final for that Parliament at least. He seems to have acquiesced very placidly in the defeat, and thenceforward his affection for Reform became less ardent than before.

In the same year we find Mr. Pitt endeavouring to improve the condition of Ireland, by shaking off those shackles which the selfishness of the commercial class in England had imposed on the sister island, and by granting the boon of free-trade to her people. Strange to say, Fox, the boasted friend of popular rights, threw himself forward as the uncompromising adversary of any such a boon. The Manchester merchants and manufacturers raised the selfish cry that, if free-trade were conceded to Ireland, they would themselves be ruined and undone. A petition, embodying these sentiments, signed by no less than 80,000 Lancashire manufacturers, was presented to the House of Commons. These men urged that the admission of Irish fustians and cottons into England was all that was wanting to annihilate the cotton trade of the country.

"There are," said Mr. Pitt,[1] "only two possible systems for countries placed in relation to each other like Great Britain and Ireland. The one, of having the smaller completely subordinate and subservient to the greater, to make the one, as it were, an instrument of advantage, and to cause all her efforts to operate in favour and conduce merely to the interest of the other; this system we had tried in respect to Ireland. . . . The other was a participation and community of benefits, and a system of equality and fairness, which, without tending to aggrandize the one or to depress the other, should seek the aggregate interest of the empire. Such a situation of commercial equality, in which there is to be a community of benefits, demands also a community of

[1] Stanhope's "Life of Pitt," vol. i. pp. 211, 212.

burdens ; and it is in this situation that I am anxious to place the two countries. . . . Adopt then . . . that system of trade with Ireland which will have tended to enrich one part of the empire without impoverishing the other, while it gives strength to both.

'It is twice blessed ;
It blesseth him that gives and him that takes.'

Surely, after the heavy loss which our country has sustained from the recent severance of her Transatlantic dominions, there ought to be no object more impressed on the feelings of the House than to endeavour to preserve from futher dismemberment and diminution—in fact, to unite and connect—what yet remains of our reduced and shattered empire. . . . Of all the objects of my political life, this is in my opinion the most important in which I have ever been engaged ; nor do I imagine I shall ever meet another that shall rouse every emotion of my heart in so strong a degree as does the present."

It was the boast of Pitt that he was the

first of public statesmen who had really read, marked, learned, and thoroughly digested the principles laid down by Adam Smith in the "Wealth of Nations," and the boast was to a certain extent justifiable, as Lord Shelburne, an earlier disciple of Smith, never had much opportunity of carrying his principles into practice. Pitt was above all things a financier, and a great one, though Mr. Lecky, in the chapter of his History which he devotes to a survey of Mr. Pitt's ministry, gives reasons for holding that his practical application of the great social philosopher's principles, so far from leading to the real prosperity of the nation, saddled the country with a debt of six millions, to say nothing of other evils—" a bitter inheritance which has descended to us and will descend to generations yet to come."

No sooner was Mr. Pitt safely established in power than he set himself, like an honest man, to work at reducing, if he could not abolish, the wholesale corruption which tainted Parliament, and more than tainted the civil service of the Crown, and especially the departments of the Customs and Excise. By throwing open all public loans to the public itself, and not reserving them and lottery tickets for a few favoured friends, he cleansed out an Augean stable of corruption. He abolished a great form of corruption by limiting the privilege of members of the two Houses of Parliament to "frank" their letters. He also put down part of the smuggling trade by lowering the duties on excisable imports; and he simplified and enforced a better system of auditing the public accounts than that which had prevailed down to his time. "It is the supreme merit of the early years of Mr. Pitt's administration that he carried order and light into this chaos, and placed the finances of the country once more on a sound basis."[1] The only form of corruption which he encouraged was the profuse distribution of peerages among his own supporters and the friends of his royal master.

It is as a consummate master of finance

---

[1] Lecky, "History of England," vol. v. pp. 20, 21.

that Pitt's name will be longest remembered ; and, as Mr. Lecky remarks, "his first and probably his greatest title to regard was his financial administration. No characteristic of his intellect appears to have more strongly impressed those who knew him than his extraordinary aptitude for all questions relating to figures ; and, having taken the office of Chancellor of the Exchequer, he gave financial measures the most prominent place in the early years of his ministry." Burke and other public men sneered at him for hunting into holes to find out and detect abuses ; but Pitt proudly declared in reply, that " he could not conceive how an English minister could consider himself justified in omitting any exertion that might tend, even in the most minute particular, to promote that economy on which the recovery of the State from its present depressed condition so much depended." "It was in this class of legislation that the true greatness of Pitt was most clearly shown. In measures of a more splendid and more imposing character he rarely was really successful, but no minister

H

displayed more industry and skill in remedying detailed abuses, discovering the causes that rendered particular branches of the revenue unproductive, introducing order, simplicity, and economy into great departments of national finance. . . . His financial statements were masterpieces of comprehensive and luminous exposition, and his great measure, in 1787, consolidating the different branches of Customs and Excise, was one of the most important in English commercial history." [1]

But, after all, a still higher credit may be claimed for Pitt on account of the commercial treaty with France, which, in spite of the strong insular antipathies of the British people, he persuaded the Parliament and the King to sanction, in 1786. He held with Lord Shelburne that it was wholly a mistake to suppose that England and France were national enemies, but that, on the contrary, it was their interest to act in concert ; and no sooner was the treaty signed by Mr. Eden at Paris than

[1] Lecky, " History of England," vol. v. pp. 33, 35.

our great manufacturing centres of industry found the advantage of having near their doors a market of more than twenty millions of purchasers for their goods. It is true that eight or nine years later the French Revolution, and the war which was its immediate result, tore this treaty up into shreds; but still, during as many years of peace, its good effects had been tested by experience.

The great object of Pitt in negotiating this treaty was to put an end, as far as possible, to prohibitions and prohibitory duties. He did not seek to reduce or endanger the revenue by abolishing the custom duties altogether. On the contrary, he expected to benefit the revenue from that source by imposing only moderate duties which would really be levied on all articles imported, and which would deal almost a death-blow on the contraband trade. For, in spite of Pitt's previous measures, the contraband trade in several of its branches continued to prevail.

"I am obliged to confess," said Pitt, in the House of Commons, "that increase of revenue by means of reduction of duties was once thought a paradox; but experience has now convinced us that it is more than practicable."

But though his commercial treaty with France was the most important measure of Pitt's public life, it cannot be denied that his contemporaries were far more inclined to worship him on account of his scheme for the reduction of the National Debt by means of a Sinking Fund. At his accession to place and power that debt stood at 250 millions; and he saw clearly that it was only in a time of peace that it could be reduced. In proposing a new loan in 1784, for the purpose of funding a part of this debt, Mr. Pitt insisted that in all operations the nation should keep in view its gradual redemption and extinction; and he gave reasons for preferring a fund at a high rate of interest to one at a low rate; and, accordingly, in 1786, when he found himself with a surplus of £900,000 in hand, and therefore at liberty to take steps in this direction, he proposed by a slight increase of taxation on one or two articles to raise that surplus to a million, and to apply this sum annually, if possible, to the extinction of the National Debt. In this step he borrowed the idea of the Rev. Dr. Price, who had published, in 1772, an " Appeal to the Public on the Subject of the National Debt," and who had strongly urged the importance of laying by a certain sum annually for that purpose, and had shown how in the course of a few years the entire debt could be discharged. But in order to effect a consummation so much to be desired, it was necessary that the nation should be at peace, not at war ; and the outbreak of a war, which seemed likely to be a protracted war, deranged all the minister's calculations, and left the nation about twenty millions out of pocket before its end. Those who are curious to see these sums worked out, and the fallacy which underlay the Sinking Fund exposed, may see the figures given in detail in the eighteenth chapter of Mr. Lecky's " History of England," who thus sums up his indictment against the great statesman :—

" The case against the financial administration of Pitt is overwhelming. During the first four or five years of the war, he committed the fatal blunder of leaving the taxation of the country almost unchanged, and raising almost the whole sum required for the war in the form of loans. In this manner, in the very beginning of the contest, when the resources of the country were still untouched, he hampered the nation with an enormous debt, which made it impossible for it by any efforts to balance its expenditure. On the other hand, in the first six years of the war, he raised by loans no less than £108,500,000, and he raised them on terms so unfavourable that they added nearly £200,000,000 to the capital of the National Debt. . . . The false error of raising so small a sum by taxation during the first years of the war has been extenuated on the ground of the unpopularity of the war, and the distress occasioned by defective harvests and by a commercial crisis of unusual severity. But the ablest defender of Pitt has candidly acknowledged that two great miscalculations profoundly influenced his financial policy. One of them was the belief, which he expressed both in public and in private, that the resources of France had been ruined by the first shock of the Revolution, and that the war which had begun was likely to be a very short one. The other was his firm conviction that in his Sinking Fund he had found a rapid and infallible instrument for reducing the National Debt. After a few years, it is true, the magnitude of the problem became evident, and the financial ability of Pitt was displayed in the new taxes which he devised. But the error of the early years of the war was not and could not be retrieved, and the consequences are felt to the present hour."

CHAPTER XI.

The King's Illness — Discussions in Parliament and in the Cabinet on a Regency Bill — Treachery of Lord Thurlow ; his Dismissal from the Chancellorship — The King's Recovery and Visit to St. Paul's to return Public Thanks — Lord Buckingham resigns the Vice-Royalty of Ireland.

WE now come suddenly to another chapter in the life of the Premier, one in which his sound sense and good fortune will be seen to have placed him as minister in a still more secure position than ever : I refer to the episode of the King's illness.

The facts, told briefly, were as follows :— Early in this summer (1788) the King became ill, and was sent in July to Cheltenham to try the effects of the waters ; but he returned to Kew and Windsor no better, but rather the worse, and (to use his own words) "grown all at once an old man." It was not, however, till the last week in October that mental disease showed its early symptoms, which, by the 5th of November, had become most formidable. In spite of his alarm and his grief, Mr. Pitt, on learning the extent of the malady, sent out expresses to summon a meeting of the Cabinet; he was almost expecting that the next day would bring the news of the King's death, but he saw also a host of difficulties before him in case the King should live on with his reason overclouded. " In such a case there were strong grounds," writes Lord Stanhope, " for imposing some restrictions on a Regency. Yet, how could such restrictions be imposed, except by an Act of Parliament ; and how could any Act of Parliament be passed without a King to give it his assent ? Thus, in one sense, a limited Regency seemed requisite, while in another sense it seemed impossible."

During the next few days the King grew still worse in body and mind, and the physicians gave the royal household reason to believe that there was little or no chance of his recovery. The Prince of Wales, seeing that the Regency, whether limited or not, would devolve on himself, sent to consult Lord Loughborough as to the constitutional course to be pursued, at the same time summoning Charles James Fox back from a tour in Italy. It would have been natural for Pitt to have consulted his own Chancellor, Thurlow, in this emergency; but Thurlow had joined in an intrigue with the Whigs to secure the highest place to which he could aspire in that party, whose star was now in the ascendant, at the cost of tripping up Lord Loughborough. Pitt was not long in taking his own course, straightforward and direct, and quite independent of both. "He would listen to no terms for himself. He would consider only his bounden duty to his afflicted King. He would, by the authority of Parliament, impose some restrictions on the Regency for a limited time, so that the Sovereign might resume his power without difficulty in case his reason were restored. What might be the just limits or the necessary period of such restrictions, he had not yet decided, and was still revolving in his mind. But he had never the least idea, as his opponents feared, of a Council of Regency which might impede the Prince in the choice of a new Administration. On the contrary, Pitt looked forward to his own immediate dismissal from the public service, and he had determined to return to the practice of his profession at the Bar." [1]

Mr. Pitt was also embarrassed by the fact that Parliament was about to reassemble, it having been prorogued only to the 20th of November, and there was no ordinary power to prorogue it beyond that date. On the meeting of the two Houses, therefore, he moved an adjournment for a fortnight, deprecating all public discussion in the interim, and suggesting that, should the King's disorder continue, the state of public affairs should be taken solemnly into consideration on the 4th of December. Meantime the King was removed, much against his will, from Windsor to Kew Palace, the physicians asserting that there

---

[1] Stanhope's "Life of Pitt," vol. i. p. 313.

was a fair prospect of his recovery in
time, and that the privacy and seclusion
of Kew was to be preferred to Windsor
for His Majesty under the existing circumstances.

On the re-assembling of Parliament, a
report was laid before the two Houses as
to the state of the King's mind, and a committee was appointed to examine the physicians in attendance on him. One of
these, Dr. Willis (who was also a clergy-
man) was from the first sanguine of his
ultimate recovery; but they all agreed that
such recovery must be a matter of time.
On the 8th of December, Fox propounded
the sentiment that there was no necessity
of appointing any committee, or of search-
ing for precedents; and that the Prince of
Wales had as much inherent right to take
the Regency of the kingdom in hand as he
would have had to succeed to the throne
in the event of the demise of the Crown.
Mr. Pitt, on the contrary, maintained that,
in the absence of any precedent, the assertion of such an inherent right in the Prince
was little short of treason, thus, it will be

seen, taking up a far less absolute position than his Whig opponent.

The country at large was not long in deciding between these rival opinions, and day by day the views of Mr. Pitt were confirmed by the public sense. On the 16th, Pitt brought forward three resolutions embodying his opinion, and had the satisfaction of seeing them carried by a large majority, in spite of the opposition of the Prince of Wales and of Fox, who lost immensely in credit by saying that Pitt " would never have proposed to limit the Prince's power, had he not been conscious that he did not possess the Prince's confidence, and would not be the Prince's minister." This unmerited taunt, and the eloquent apostrophe of the Lord Chancellor: "When I forget my King, may my God forget me," doubtless helped largely to bring about this result, the more so because the public were quite unaware of the tricks to which Lord Thurlow had stooped in order to secure the Great Seal.

The third resolution proposed and carried by Mr. Pitt enabled the Lord

Chancellor, supported by a vote of the two Houses, to put the Great Seal to a commission for giving the royal assent to the intended Bill. The resolutions, in spite of the strong opposition from the Prince's friends, were carried by a majority of three to two in the House of Lords.

In the following month of February (1789), when the Regency Bill was about to be read a third time in the House of Lords, the country was surprised and gladdened by learning that the health of the King was slowly returning. The Bill was, therefore, postponed *sine die;* and on the 23rd, Mr. Pitt had an interview with the King, and was satisfied that there was no reason why he should not resume the discharge of his public duties. The Bill, therefore, fell to the ground ; and a spontaneous illumination of London, followed by a visit of the King, Queen, and Royal Family in state to St. Paul's to join in a public thanksgiving service, helped to blot it out from the memory of the public. Lord Macaulay rightly regards the day of this service as marking the zenith of Pitt's political career. " To such an extraordinary height of power and glory," he writes, " had this extraordinary man risen at twenty-nine years of age."

There can be no doubt that during these eventful months of strife, Mr. Pitt, to use a current phrase, " scored " highly over his opponents, who made mistake upon mistake, and sank accordingly in the estimate of the country. He had an uphill battle to fight, the more so because of the tendency in human nature to worship the rising rather than the setting sun. His consummate skill and unconquerable firmness, however, were the main causes of the victory. But had his opponents been well generalled, the majority at his command might have collapsed, and the restrictions which he thought needful might never have been imposed.

Lord North, in the debate on the 16th of December, spoke strongly against the proposal of the Government; and Fox, in one of his most able speeches, bitterly denounced the measure. Fox, however, was guilty of a most unnecessary and unjustifiable piece of slander on the character of his rival, who, he said (as stated above), "would never have proposed any limitation on the Prince's power, had he not been conscious that he did not deserve the Prince's confidence, and that he would not be the Prince's minister." "I declare," said Pitt, "the attack which the right honourable gentleman has just now made to be unfounded, arrogant, and presumptuous. As to my being conscious that I do not deserve the favour of the Prince, I can only say that I know but one way in which I or any other man could deserve it, by having uniformly endeavoured in a public situation to do my duty to the King his father, and the country at large." Pitt added, with proper spirit, that if, in thus endeavouring to deserve the confidence of the Prince, it should appear that he, in fact, had lost it, however mortifying that circumstance might be to him, he should certainly regret, but at the same time it was impossible that he should ever repent of it.

Further than this, it is now generally known that had not the Opposition created so many obstructions and delays, in all probability the Prince would have been installed as Regent at Christmas, 1788, or else very early in the new year; and that the King, in that case, on his recovery, would have refused to resume his sceptre. Had this happened, and had Fox and his allies taken possession of Downing Street, a large part of Pitt's followers would have gone over to the opposite camp; and had Pitt then been recalled to office by the King, he would have come back shorn of a considerable part of his supporters.

It is a pleasing and eloquent proof of the general approval which Mr. Pitt's conduct received that, whilst these controversies were proceeding, a meeting of the bankers and merchants of London was held, at which it was proposed to bestow on him a free gift of £100,000—a gift which, however, he firmly declined to accept.

It was fortunate indeed for the King and the Royal Family that they had in Pitt such a staunch and devoted champion, determined, as he undoubtedly was, to protect the interests of the King, so that, in the event of the return of his mental powers, his royal authority and his private interests should alike be recovered in an unimpaired condition. Pitt well knew that unless restrictions were placed on the powers of the Prince of Wales, serious encroachments on the rights of the Sovereign would be made, and he guarded the cause of the afflicted King with never-ceasing watchfulness and care. He recommended that the management of his royal master, and all appointments to positions in the household, should be placed in the hands of the Queen ; and though he proposed to confer on the Prince Regent full power of choosing his own ministers, still he desired the imposition of some restrictions upon the disposal of the King's property, whether civil or personal, and also on the granting of pensions or places in reversion. It was his wish, also, that the Prince of Wales should not have, during the King's illness, the right to bestow peerages, except on such of His Majesty's issue as might attain the age of twenty-one.

There has rarely been more of court intrigue or political scheming than that which prevailed among the ministers of the Crown during the illness of the King. Pitt had not only to contend against the acknowledged partizans of the Prince of Wales, but he had also to be on his guard against some of the members of his own Cabinet. Lord Thurlow, who was then Lord Chancellor, rendered himself peculiarly obnoxious and dangerous to Pitt during this season of trial and anxiety. Although Lord Thurlow had naturally taken a conspicuous part in the plan—which had been drawn up by the ministers and approved of by both Houses of Parliament—for conducting the government of the country during the King's affliction, it is a fact that on the day when the Regency Bill was to be debated in the House of Lords, Mr. Pitt was not sure whether the Lord Chancellor would support or oppose him. It was afterwards discovered, beyond doubt, that Lord Thurlow was in the habit of conferring with the Prince of Wales, to whom he communicated the course of action which the Government had decided to adopt, thereby affording the Opposition

the great advantage of knowing the plans
of the ministers beforehand, and of enabling them to take measures of the most
effectual hostility. Yet Lord Thurlow was
the man who, with lofty mien and swagger-
ing language, declared publicly that the
unlimited powers which the Opposition
sought to confer upon the Prince almost
amounted to treason against the royal
authority. It has been said that Lord
Thurlow's fit of loyalty was the result of
the unexpected improvement in the King's
health, though, when the King's recovery
appeared hopeless, he began to consider
whether he might not retain the Great Seal
under a Regency. He formed a part of
Mr. Pitt's government for several years,
but it was said of him that he opposed
everything and proposed nothing. Indeed,
he opposed Mr. Pitt's Sinking Fund Bill,
when it was before the House of Lords, in
such contemptuous terms, that Pitt wrote
to the King asking whether His Majesty
would part with his Lord Chancellor or his
First Lord of the Treasury. The King
without hesitation answered the question

in Mr. Pitt's favour, telling Lord Thurlow that he had no longer any need of his services.

It was the general opinion that the Government would be immediately changed on the passing of the Regency Bill. The retirement from office of the minister who, in the space of five years, had raised the country's finances from the deplorable condition to which the American War had reduced them, to a state of prosperity never before known, was regarded with apprehension and dismay. "Amidst the prolonged and desperate struggles for pre-eminence," writes Dean Pellew, "which occurred between the rival parties, hope at length began to whisper that the *casus belli* was no longer the same, and that a merciful Providence, unobserved by the combatants, was gradually removing the ground and subject-matter of contention."

With respect to the much-debated question of the Regency during the King's mental illness, and the terms and conditions upon which it should be conferred on the Prince of Wales, Pitt took the more sen-

sible, and, as it happened, the more fortunate
side.   To use the words of his biographer,
Gifford :—[1]

"The great constitutional points which
the discussions on the Regency involved,
the important precedent which they went
to establish, and the opportunity which
they afforded for displaying the firmness
and consistency of Mr. Pitt's character in
a novel and interesting point of view, all
combine to render this an important epoch
in his parliamentary and political life.   It
has been often remarked that, on this
occasion, Mr. Pitt, who had lately stood
forth the champion of prerogative, proclaimed himself the asserter of popular
rights ; while Mr. Fox, who had been distinguished as the man of the people, appeared as the advocate of claims hostile to
those rights.   As applied to Mr. Pitt, the
remark is neither totally just nor totally
unjust.   He certainly supported the rights
of Parliament, but not in opposition to the
prerogatives of the Crown ; on the con-

[1] Vol. i. p. 403.

trary, all his efforts had for their object to prevent the Crown from being stript of any of its lawful appendages, more than it was absolutely necessary to invest in the Regent, for the exercise and support of the royal authority; and to secure to the Sovereign the certain means of resuming the kingly power, in its utmost plenitude, whenever that incapacity should cease, the existence of which could alone justify the transfer of any portion of it to another. But, even here, constitutionally speaking, he was the supporter of popular rights; for he well knew, with every sound statesman and lawyer who had flourished since the Revolution, that the prerogative of the Crown is an essential part of the rights of the people, which it tends to confirm and secure."

And again, recurring to the subject, he comments thus :—

" The part which Mr. Pitt had to sustain, at this important period, was a part of extreme difficulty; every step he took exposed him to suspicions the most grating to a generous and noble mind, and to reproaches which he would have shuddered to deserve. Every measure which a sense of duty led him to adopt, subjected him to imputations of interested motives, which his soul abhorred, and, while he consulted exclusively the rights of the Crown, and the welfare of the country, he incurred the odious accusation of considering only the promotion of his own views, and the gratification of his own ambition. All the arts of ingenious sophistry ; all the ridicule of inventive, but distorted genius ; all the invectives of impotent malice, and all the taunts of malignant enmity, combined to produce that mental irritation which is most favourable to attack, and most hostile to defence. But the combination was vain as the rage of the winds which assail the monarch of our woods. Its fury was spent in fruitless efforts to shake that firmness, which could only be moved by the desolation of Europe and the calamities of the country. His conduct was the more deserving of praise, as its certain consequence was his dismission from office, by the Regent, at a time too when his fortune was impaired, and his circumstances were impoverished, by unavoidable inattention to his personal concerns, resulting from the magnitude and extent of his official duty."[1]

In the course of this year (1789), Mr. Pitt was pained by Lord Buckingham resigning the Lord-Lieutenancy of Ireland, partly on the plea of ill-health, but partly also because the King refused to raise him to a Dukedom, in spite of Mr. Pitt's strong request to that effect. Mr. Pitt, however, contrived to carry on the government of the three kingdoms in spite of the secession of the noble head of all the Temples and all the Grenvilles, formidable as they were at that time by the clannish zeal with which they supported each other, both in and out of Parliament.

> " Illos
> Defendit numerus, junctœque umbone phalanges."

Twenty years later, indeed, after Mr. Pitt's death, Mr. William Grenville was called by the King to undertake the Premiership, and he held the post of First

[1] Vol. i. p. 405.

Lord of the Treasury for a few months as
head of " the Ministry of all the Talents."
But a great deal was about to occur before then, including the death of William
Pitt himself.

CHAPTER XII.

Outburst of the Revolution in France—Attitude of Mr. Pitt towards its Leaders—Wilberforce and West Indian Slavery—Pitt opposes the Repeal of the Test Act and Parliamentary Reform — Pitt's Budget — He is offered the Order of the Garter—His Legislation for Canada—First Symptoms of the Decay of Pitt's Power—His Letter to the Archbishop of Canterbury on Tithe Commutation.

IT will have been observed by the reader that up to this point scarcely any mention has been made of France, her sovereign and her people, with the exception of the brief episode of Mr. Pitt's visit to that country in 1784, when he saw Louis XVI. and his Queen, Marie Antoinette, amid all the meridian splendour of the French Court.

But six years had passed since that

visit, and now quite another spirit had arisen in France. For many generations a gulf had been widening between the nobles and the people. The former imposed the taxes, from which they were free themselves to a large extent; and the lower classes had to pay them. There was but little intermarriage between the blue blood of the aristocracy and the mass of the people; and the country stood divided into two opposite camps. A great and disastrous change had been long foreseen and prophesied by such far-sighted men as Rousseau and Lord Chesterfield; and a mighty storm had been long gathering, though its signs were little heeded by the world at large.

It would be impossible here to give an account of the rise and progress of this European storm, so well known as the first French Revolution. The States General of France, a body answering in the main to our House of Commons, had not been convened for more than a century and a half; and when the people, growing, or rather grown, conscious of their strength, insisted on its being allowed to meet—May 5th, 1789—that body speedily proclaimed itself " The National Assembly." On the 14th of July following, the people rose in arms against both the King and the nobles, stormed and took the state prison of the Bastille, putting its garrison to death. And further, on the 4th of August, intoxicated with their success, the raw legislators of this Assembly swept away by a single vote the privileges of the clergy, the nobility, and the provinces. One success soon led to other efforts, and again on October 5th the mob marched in arms to Versailles, where they broke into the palace, and brought back the King and Queen, virtually as their prisoners, to Paris, of which thenceforth the mob became the supreme ruler.

It was natural that those Englishmen who preferred progress and liberty to ancient customs, traditions, and privileges, should view this novel outbreak in different lights. To Charles James Fox and Sheridan the events in Paris, including the destruction of the Bastille, approved themselves ; and Fox declared the last-named event the " greatest " and " best " that had happened in the history of the world. The more philosophic natures of Burke and of Windham, though they were sincere lovers of liberty, did not care for that boon when separated from the sacred cause of justice ; and the great mass of the country gentlemen who composed the House of Commons, and the members of the House of Lords, with very few exceptions, regarded the outbreak in Paris as the very incarnation of wickedness. Doubtless they feared that such an outbreak would prove contagious, and that the events of 1789 in Paris would repeat themselves in London in the following year. But when the King opened Parliament at Westminster in January, 1790, he was made to say, with studied moderation, that " the affairs of the Continent had engaged his most serious attention ; " and Mr. Pitt showed no symptoms of alarm, nor did he even propose an increase in the Army Estimates. He took a sober and hopeful view of the situation, and thus expressed himself :—

"The present convulsions of France must sooner or later terminate in general harmony and regular order; and though such a situation may make her more formidable, it may also make her less obnoxious as a neighbour. I wish for the restoration of tranquillity in that country, although it appears to me to be distant. Whenever her system shall have become restored, if it shall prove freedom rightly understood, freedom resulting from good order and good government, France will stand forth as one of the most brilliant Powers in Europe. Nor can I regard with envious eyes any approximation in neighbouring states to those sentiments which are the characteristics of every British subject."[1]

From these words it will be seen that Mr. Pitt's first impressions of the French revolutionary movement were not based on panic, or on any slavish adherence to the doctrine of "the divine right of kings."

[1] Speech, Feb. 9th, 1790, quoted by Lord Stanhope, "Life of Pitt," vol. i. p. 357.

About this time (March) an insult offered to the British flag abroad, known as the Nootka Sound affair, led to a threat of declaring war against Spain, and a vote was carried in the House of Commons for a million in order to defray its cost.

" ' The country at this moment,' Mr. Pitt might well conclude, 'is in a state of prosperity far greater than at any period, even the most flourishing, before the late war; and this I can incontestably prove from a comparative view of the exports and imports of that period compared with those of the present '—so fully and so rapidly had the loss of the American colonies, deemed irreparable by all our wisest statesmen, been repaired. Such," writes Lord Stanhope, " was the picture which the Prime Minister could draw in April, 1790." [1]

In the same month Wilberforce moved for leave to bring in a Bill to prevent the further importation of slaves into our West Indian Colonies. The debate lasted two nights, but though Pitt and Fox put forth

---

[1] Stanhope's " Life of Pitt," vol. i. p. 383.

all their powers, for once on the same side, in its support, the Bill was lost by a large majority. In the course of the same session Mr. Pitt opposed Fox's motion for the repeal of the Test Act, on the ground that though Nonconformists might well claim toleration and the protection of the law for their tenets, they could not claim perfect equality without endangering the Established Church ; and that the usual act of indemnity, which had been annually renewed, in their favour, was sufficient for all practical purposes. The Bill was rejected by 294 votes to 105.

Soon after this division the Reform question was again brought forward. Mr. Flood proposed a resolution in favour of amending the representation of the people, with a view to make it more adequate to the growth and the changed circumstances of the constituencies. The opposition to this motion was led by Mr. W. Windham, who objected to "the repairing of one's house in the hurricane season," alluding to the revolution which had commenced in France. Mr. Pitt, though he acknowledged that the motion was substantially the same as that which he had himself brought forward a few years before, declined to support it now on the ground that the present was an unsuitable time for bringing it forward, though at a future and more convenient season he "certainly meant again to submit his own ideas on the subject to the House." Finding that the general feeling of the House was against him, Mr. Flood withdrew his motion.

On the 10th of June the Parliament was prorogued, after having lasted six years, and was almost immediately dissolved; and the country at large being satisfied with the steady progress which had been made under the existing government, the election passed off without excitement, and Mr. Pitt became stronger than ever.

Mr. Fitzherbert, afterwards Lord St. Helen's, was sent out to Madrid as Ambassador, to demand reparation for the outrage mentioned above; thanks to the firmness of Great Britain, an appeal to arms was avoided, and the year ended in peace, as it had begun.

But the relations between this country and France still continued to be critical, and such as to absorb the attention and care of Mr. Pitt. The King, feeling a natural sympathy with his brother of France, was much more of an alarmist than his minister, of whom then it might be said with truth,—

> " Justum ac tenacem propositi virum
> Non civium ardor prava jubentium
> Mente quatit solidâ."

Throughout 1790 the National Assembly continued to hold its sittings in Paris, and to it must be given the credit of having reformed some abuses and of having introduced some salutary reforms, though they had swept away much that was at once most venerable and useful.

Edmund Burke, who had been hitherto known as a moderate Liberal, now took up his brilliant pen against France, and produced his " Reflections on the French Revolution," in which he showed the dangerous character of its principles. Pitt, however, in spite of the excitement caused by the open avowal of Republican sentiments in London by Dr. Price, Tom Paine, and others of that school, refused to take any strong line in the way of opposition or censure, and sought rather to guide the movement into safe courses.

Lord Stanhope writes thus in his " Life of Pitt ":—[1]

" While condemning the excesses of the French Revolution, even at that early period, and apprehending its results, Pitt never lost the hope that among the friends of that Revolution the more moderate party might prevail. In public he held forth as the rule of his administration strict neutrality as to the internal contests; in private he moreover sought, through divers and not only in diplomatic channels, to exchange pacific explanations with the leaders of the popular party ; and he was determined to maintain against all obstacles, as long as possible, that peace so essential to the welfare of his country, and on which depended his own course of financial retrenchments and reforms."

[1] Vol. i. p. 374.

About this time, in the hope of neutralizing the wayward temper of his uncongenial colleague, Lord Chancellor Thurlow, Mr. Pitt raised his own kinsman, William Grenville, to a peerage, giving him at the same time the leadership of the House of Lords—a step which did not please all his party.

The first session of the new Parliament witnessed some important debates. In December, Mr. Pitt brought forward his Budget, no longer, like that of the previous April, a Budget of unmixed prosperity, for he was forced to include in it a sum of nearly three millions and a quarter for what was and is known to history as "The Russian Armament." Not anxious to leave this as a permanent addition to the National Debt, he proposed to spread it over four years, imposing some taxes of a temporary nature on spirits, sugar, malt, and other articles, and to appropriate to its repayment half a million of unclaimed dividends in the hands of the Bank of England, a sum which the directors in the end agreed to lend to the Government without interest. On this occasion he seems to have put forth all his powers of oratory. The following is an extract from the diary of his friend Wilberforce :—

"*22nd Dec.*—At the House till past two. Pitt's astonishing speech. This was almost the finest speech Pitt ever delivered : it was one which you would say at once he never could have made if he had not been a mathematician. He put things by as he proceeded, and then returned to the very point from which he had started, with the most astonishing clearness. He had all the lawyers against him, but carried a majority of the House mainly by the force of his speech. It pleased Burke prodigiously. 'Sir,' he said, 'the right hon. gentleman and I have often been opposed to one another, but his speech to-night has neutralized my opposition ; nay, sir, he has dulcified me.'"

The impeachment of Warren Hastings was another difficulty. The question was raised whether the recent dissolution of Parliament did or did not virtually put an end to it. The lawyers were equally divided on the question ; but there was a great concurrence of opinion within the walls of Parliament that the trial should go on ; Mr. Pitt took the latter view, and his view prevailed. Dean Pellew thus writes :—[1]

"This question furnished the only occasions on which, as Lord Sidmouth believed, Mr. Pitt and Mr. Fox were ever brought together in private life. They met at a consultation held in December, 1790, to consider, with reference to the trial of Mr. Warren Hastings, whether an impeachment by the Commons was abated by a dissolution of Parliament. Mr. Pitt and Mr. Fox agreed in thinking that it was not, and nothing could exceed the ease and cordiality of their manners towards each other on that occasion."

Accordingly, the trial was condemned to "drag its slow length along" for several years, though some persons thought, or affected to think, that "the ardour of politics might overcome the slowness of the law," and hasten it to an issue.

[1] "Life of Lord Sidmouth," vol. i. p. 80.

Just before Christmas the King offered the blue riband of the Garter to Mr. Pitt, and, indeed, pressed on him its acceptance, but he declined the honour; and, at a mere expression of his wish, the King bestowed it on his brother, Lord Chatham.[1]

In the course of this session Mr. Pitt brought in a Bill for the better government of Canada, which still remained faithful to Great Britain in spite of the loss of the rest of our American colonies. He proposed to divide the province into two parts, under the denominations of Upper and Lower Canada; the Upper for the English and American settlers, the Lower for the French Canadians, with a local legislature to each part. "This division," said Pitt, "could, I hope, be made in such a manner as to give each a great majority in their own particular share, although it cannot be expected to draw a line of complete separation." He also proposed to enable the Crown to grant hereditary titles in the province of Canada, and to appro-

[1] Jesse's "Memoirs of George III.," vol. iii. p. 140.

priate certain lands as a provision for the clergy of the Church of England there. It is worthy of note that on this occasion, though he opposed certain portions of the Bill, Fox thus prophetically expressed himself, in words which have since been often quoted in reference to another of our dependencies: "*I am convinced that the only method of retaining distant colonies with advantage is to enable them to govern themselves.*" It is perhaps also worthy of note that this measure caused the final rupture of the friendship which had existed between Fox and Burke, and that the latter became still more isolated in the political world than ever, owing to his almost frantic denunciations of the Revolution in France, the good points of which, as well as its dangers, struck most forcibly the statesmanlike mind of Pitt, who, when appealed to in the debates, while extolling Burke's patriotism, advised him, instead of attacking the French Constitution, to extol that of Great Britain.

This same session is remarkable also for having witnessed the agreement of Pitt and his great rival Fox in at all events one benevolent and beneficial measure, so far as it went, brought in by Mr. Mitford, afterwards Lord Redesdale, to exempt such Roman Catholics as should take a certain oath which it presented from most of the various penalties and disabilities imposed on them under the Penal Laws of the previous centuries, though it did not go so far as to allow them to take their seats in Parliament. That measure had yet to wait forty years for a " convenient season."

Up to this date, the middle of the session of 1791, the career of Mr. Pitt has been eminently successful. He has asserted all along his mastery and supremacy over the counsels of Parliament, and, though strongly and even stoutly opposed at times, he has triumphed over all opposition, doubtless to a very great extent because he was so strongly supported by the private favour of his friend, the King. But now appear the first signs of the little cloud on the horizon which is about to overshadow his later days. It arose in the shape of the Russian Question. When

Russia and Austria, aided by Sweden, joined hands in 1788 to make war against Turkey, Mr. Pitt had steered this country clear of actual entanglement, contenting himself with the task of striving to maintain the balance of power in Europe, and with this object he tried to enlist Holland and Prussia in a joint remonstrance, and to detach the Danes from their alliance with the two Emperors. In this Mr. Pitt was successful; but when he subsequently attempted to remonstrate with Russia, and, his remonstrances being haughtily rejected by the Empress Catharine and the Court of St. Petersburg, he asked Parliament for an increase in our naval forces, in view of the possibility of a war against Russia, he found that such a step was not approved by the public, and therefore was obliged to "sound a retreat." The "Russian Armament," after having thrown the political world into confusion at home, was quietly abandoned. "Mr. Pitt," writes Lord Stanhope,[1] "could look back with

[1] "Life of Pitt," vol. i. p. 406.

gratification to the three Allies. He was proud to think that they had been able to arrest the progress of Denmark in the North ; next to curb the ambition of Austria, and compel her to renounce the conquests she had already made. . . . It was his opinion that precisely the same course should be pursued towards Russia. But the negotiations with that view, conducted through the autumn and winter, proved altogether unsatisfactory." The session passed away without leaving any great record behind it, excepting a few changes in the *personnel* of Mr. Pitt's colleagues, scarcely worth particularizing here. At the close of it, Mr. Pitt went off to Somersetshire, to spend a few weeks' holiday with his mother at Burton Pynsent, which had the advantage of being not far from Weymouth, where the King was passing the autumn.

Towards the close of this year, Mr. Pitt addressed a long letter to the Archbishop of Canterbury, Dr. Moore, suggesting the outlines of a measure for the general commutation of tithes throughout the country, adding his opinion that "any proposal which aims at obviating the present complaints, and at the same time securing the interests of the Church, should engage the early attention of those who wish well to the Establishment, in order that they may be enabled to give a proper direction to the business if it can be put into any practicable shape." No reply from the Archbishop has been found among Mr. Pitt's papers, so in all probability the matter was allowed silently to drop on the principle of *quieta non movere*, so dear to prelates of all churches. But it seems right and only fair to place on record here the farsightedness of Mr. Pitt, whose proposal in the main was carried out with general assent and with excellent results some forty years later.

CHAPTER XIII.

THROUGHOUT the whole of 1791 the eyes of England, and indeed of Europe, were fixed on France. The death of Mirabeau, who seemed destined to guide the course of the Revolution into safer and better channels, in April of that year, left the mob without a leader able to restrain its passions. On the 21st of June the King and Queen set out secretly from Paris, where they were practically prisoners, in the hope of crossing the French bound-aries and taking refuge with a friendly ally; but they were arrested at Varennes.

An effort was made on the Continent, by the " Declaration of Pilnitz," to rouse all Europe to take up arms for the deliverance of the unfortunate Louis ; but Mr. Pitt, though desirous to see a better state of things arising in France, refused to assist with men or even with a loan or subsidy.[1] About the same time the unpopularity of Dr. Priestley, a Unitarian minister at Birmingham, who had warmly espoused the Republican cause, resulted in a riot, the burning of his house, and a large destruction of property. This threw the whole country into a ferment, which was allayed only by Dr. Priestley's embarking for the United States. Lord Stanhope writes :[2] " As in France the Revolutionary leaders ascribed every evil that befel them to the villainous machinations of Pitt, so did their friends in England not scruple to declare that the Birmingham riots had been purposely stirred up by the same abominable statesman ! " Thus the poet Coleridge,

[1] Tomline's " Life of Pitt," vol. iii. p. 440.
[2] " Life of Pitt," vol. i. p. 428.

then one of that party, begins a sonnet as
follows :—

"Though, roused by that dark Vizier, riot rude
Have driv'n our Priestley o'er the ocean swell"

How absurdly untrue such charges were,
will be inferred from the Budget which
Mr. Pitt brought forward at the opening
of the session of 1792, when, so far from
contemplating hostile measures against
France, he asked the House to vote a less
force of soldiers than in the previous year,
and also designed to carry into effect other
reductions, of which it would have been
madness to dream in the face of impend-
ing war.

Indeed, in spite of all that had happened
in the French capital, and of all that
Edmund Burke had written upon it, up to
this time at all events Mr. Pitt was sanguine that the course of events would be
overruled for the good even of that unfortunate country itself. How sanguine
he was on this head we may learn from
Dean Pellew.[1] Mr. Pitt, of whom Ad-

[1] " Life of Lord Sidmouth," vol. i. p. 72.

dington used to say he was "the most sanguine man he ever knew," was long unconvinced of the magnitude of the danger from the French Revolution; in proof of which opinion we have the following anecdote :—

After Burke's breach with Fox, Pitt invited him for the first time to dine with him. Lord Grenville, Burke, Addington, and Pitt constituted the party. After dinner Burke was earnestly representing the danger which threatened this country from the contagion of French principles, when Pitt said, " Never fear, Mr. Burke ; depend on it we shall go on as we are until the day of judgment." " Very likely, sir," replied Mr. Burke ; " it is the day of *no* judgment that I am afraid of."

On the 17th of February Mr. Pitt opened his Budget with a speech which elicited the praises even of Fox, giving a very satisfactory condition of the state of the public finances, and admitting of a repeal of several unwelcome and unpopular taxes. It is said that this was the occasion on which, if we may believe his friend

L

Addington, he "got up the Budget in two hours at Lord Arden's." It was in this speech that he paid his well-known tribute to Adam Smith.

Early in this year an association was formed, entitled "The Friends of the People," for the purpose of carrying a reform in the representation and of shortening Parliaments; the association included Sheridan and Grey, but not Fox. On notice being given of the subject being brought forward in the House, Pitt was not well, and wished to refrain from speaking. Dundas said, "What? Pitt not speak? but he *must* speak." Mr. Pitt did make a speech, which has been considered one of his best. The gist of it was that, though he was still as anxious as ever to see improvements made in the representative system which would bring it practically into more perfect harmony with the theory of the Constitution, yet he would never, for the sake of a theory, expose the State to danger by seeking to effect reforms at an unreasonable time, "when treason is abroad in the very air."

In the same session (April 2nd), Mr. Pitt spoke most earnestly and forcibly, along with his rival Fox, in favour of Mr. Wilberforce's motion for the immediate abolition of the slave trade; and Lord Stanhope tells us that this was "one of the greatest speeches that he ever made." In spite of this speech, however, his friend Wilberforce was defeated by more than three to two. On this occasion Pitt's eloquence perfectly thrilled the House, and doubtless helped to swell his majority. During the closing part he seemed to be "inspired," and Lord Auckland declared it "the finest display of eloquence in the recollection of the country." [1]

The day on which Pitt was to be put upon his trial, however, was now approaching. The French Revolution, which, as we have seen, commenced in May, 1789, was now about to reach its culminating point in the imprisonment of the French King and his beautiful Queen in the Temple and in their execution by the guillotine.

[1] " Correspondence," vol. ii. p. 400.

At the first Pitt was much averse to war, and so indeed was the King; but when the admiration of French principles ceased to be speculative in this country, and began to translate itself into open acts, the public conscience was offended and alarmed, and this offence and alarm were not quelled, but increased, by Burke's celebrated work on "The French Revolution." There were, of course, those who, with Fox, Sheridan, and Grey, most deeply and sincerely regretted that the principles of the Revolution should be condemned in this land of freedom; and there were others who thought that Pitt would have been justified in proclaiming openly a holy war against a people so dangerous to the peace of Europe. But Mr. Pitt was content to steer a middle course, avoiding war so long as it could be avoided consistently with the national honour, but not shrinking from drawing the sword if ever, and whenever, the need should arise.

This year witnessed also the renewal of Fox's Libel Bill, which was strongly supported by Pitt, and passed the House of

Commons with ease, though opposed in the House of Peers by Lord Thurlow. After a five nights' debate in the Upper House, it was carried by a majority of nearly two to one. " Fox and Pitt," writes Macaulay, " are fairly entitled to divide the high honour of having added to our Statute Book the inestimable law which places the liberty of the press under the protection of justice."

In this session Mr. Pitt proposed and carried another important measure; namely, a Bill enacting, in the cause of the public credit, that every newly contracted loan should be accompanied by its own sinking fund. This was to be effected by a provision that one per cent., besides the dividends on the new stock, should be paid to the Commissioners for the Reduction of the National Debt.

CHAPTER XIV.

Negotiations for widening the Ministry—Pitt appointed Warden of the Cinque Ports— His Neutrality towards France—Renewal of the Reform Question—Deprecated and opposed by Pitt as unseasonable—" The Rights of Man "—The Militia called out —Rupture with France.

AMONG the negotiations incident to the removal of Lord Thurlow was one for the admission into the Cabinet of the moderate Whigs, under Fox, the Duke of Portland and Edmund Burke ; but it fell through, Fox declining to serve, unless Pitt should first resign the premiership.

On the 5th of August died the Earl of Guilford, better known in these pages as Lord North ; and his death placed the Lord Wardenship of the Cinque Ports, and with it the ownership for life of Walmer

Castle, in the hands of the King, who at once resolved to bestow it on his favourite minister.

Mr. Pitt communicated the news to his friend Wilberforce in the following words :—

" Immediately upon Lord Guilford's death, the King has written to me in the most gracious terms, to say that he cannot let the Wardenship of the Cinque Ports go to any one except myself. Under all the present circumstances, and in the manner in which the offer came, I have no hesitation in accepting it, and I believe you will think I have done right."

Before the end of the summer Mr. Pitt took actual possession of Walmer Castle ; and in company with Mr. Addington, then Speaker, who was his guest, he was entertained at a public dinner by the Mayor and Corporation of Canterbury. There is no reason for supposing that Pitt, in spite of his fondness for port wine, often exceeded the bounds of moderation ; but the *Morning Chronicle*, in recording the fact, added that the Chancellor of the Exchequer, in walking to his carriage after dinner, "oscillated like his own Bills." Pitt grew much attached to Walmer, and most of his happiest days, as we shall see presently, were spent by him here to the end of his life.

It was now evident that Pitt was firmly decided not to interfere with France, for in the Budget which he brought forward at the opening of Parliament in January, he not only predicted peace, but at the same time he proposed some important reductions in the taxation of the country. He stated that the revenue had been constantly increasing, owing to the national prosperity, the average for the last four years being £16,200,000, or £400,000 in excess of the annual expenditure for the same period. He therefore proposed to add £200,000 a year to the Sinking Fund, and to take off taxes to the same amount. The taxes which he decided to repeal were the additional tax laid upon malt in the previous year, the taxes upon female servants, carts, and wagons, houses having less than seven windows, and the last halfpenny per pound upon candles. Indeed, the public credit was so high at this period that it was Pitt's intention to propose a reduction of the Four per Cents. to Three and a half per Cents.

In the course of this session, Grey, Sheridan, and other statesmen of advanced opinions again pressed forward the question of Parliamentary Reform. To such a reform, in itself, as we have already seen, Mr. Pitt was not only not opposed, but most favourably inclined ; but he felt and saw the wisdom of choosing a time of peace, and not of imminent war, for any experiment in that direction. Accordingly, in the following May, he opposed Mr. Grey's motion for referring to a committee various petitions in favour of Parliamentary Reform on the ground that, although he had previously supported well-considered reforms, the excesses of the French Revolutionists had altered his mind ; and that the spread of Jacobin principles in England had showed how contagious was the example of France. Such being the case, he was afraid to let slip the dogs of Parliamentary

Reform, lest he should be unable to hold in check the more ardent spirits who desired further alterations, and lest, while he sanctioned moderate changes, he should suddenly find himself let in for the approval of universal suffrage. "My plan," urged Mr. Pitt, "goes to give vigour and stability to the ancient principles of the Constitution, and not to introduce into it any new principles ; whereas the plan advocated by Mr. Grey, if really carried out to its full length, would land us on the ground of the French Republic." "I retain my opinion," he said,[1] "of the propriety of a reform in Parliament, if it can be obtained without mischief or danger. But I confess that I am not sanguine enough to hope that a reform at this time can be safely attempted. . . . At this time, and on this subject, every rational man has two things to consider : these are the probability of success, and the risk to be run by the attempt. Looking at it in both views, I see nothing but discouragement.

[1] Speech, April 30th, 1793.

I see no chance of succeeding in the first place; and I do see great danger of anarchy and confusion in the second." In all probability when he spoke thus, he knew better than most of his hearers how little chance there was of persuading the obstinate old King to adopt his views; and without the concurrence of the monarch he foresaw but too truly certain failure. The motion was accordingly rejected by the House by the great majority of 282 votes against only 41 in its favour. The question was thus shelved, never to be again introduced into Parliament until long after Mr. Pitt had been consigned to his grave.

Meantime matters were going from bad to worse in France. The other Powers of Europe recalled their ministers from Paris on the suspension of the kingly office and the formal imprisonment of Louis XVI. One of the last to be recalled was the British Ambassador, Lord Gower, who quitted France with an assurance of neutrality on the part of his master; and as a further proof of Mr. Pitt's desire to preserve peace, the French Ambassador was allowed to remain on in London, though his functions were at an end. In September followed the newly summoned National Convention, and the Republican armies having gained many successes, the nation, in its pride and fury, voted to bring the King to trial. Even a few days before that decree was published, we find Mr. Pitt still hopeful and sanguine of averting actual hostilities ; at all events, on November 19th he wrote thus to his colleague, Lord Gower (now Lord Stafford), summoning him to a Cabinet Council in the midst of "a situation both delicate and critical." "Perhaps," he added, "some opening may arise which may enable us to contribute to the termination of the war between different Powers in Europe, leaving France (which I believe is the best way) to arrange its own internal affairs as it can."

The situation was rendered most critical at home by several outbreaks in our larger towns, where the principles of the French Revolutionists were avowed and their cries echoed back. Tom Paine was made the subject of a criminal prosecution for publishing his book on "The Rights of Man," was convicted in his absence, and was outlawed accordingly. On the 1st of December was issued a royal proclamation, calling out a part of the militia, and summoning Parliament to meet at the end of a fortnight. The ministers brought forward an Alien Bill, laying for the first time disabilities on all foreigners in England, and other Bills restraining the export of arms, ammunition, and corn. Fox moved the acknowledgment of the new French Republic, and the sending an accredited minister to Paris, but he found himself in a hopeless minority. The Duke of Portland and other moderate members of the Opposition came over to the support of Mr. Pitt, and so did Lord Loughborough, succeeding Thurlow in the Great Seal. But suddenly the whole circumstances were altered by the mock trial of the King, and his execution by the guillotine on January 21st, 1793. This was followed by an order from the King in Council commanding the French representative to quit England within eight days ; and before the expiration of that time, the French Government took the final step of declaring war against England and Holland. Thus the last chances of peace being gone, the trumpets on both sides were sounded for war.

CHAPTER XV.

England forced into War against France—Murders of Louis XVI. and of Marie Antoinette — Seditious Meetings and Publications in England—Pitt obtains the Support of the Moderate Whigs—Accession of the Duke of Portland, Lord Spencer, and Windham, etc.

WITH the declaration of war by France against England in February, 1793, ends the first half, and by far the more glorious half, of Mr. Pitt's political career. During the previous ten years, any intimate friend could have addressed to him the words of Horace to the Emperor Augustus :—

"Cum tot sustineas et tanta negotia solus."

And, in spite of the opposition of Fox, Sheridan, and Grey, Mr. Pitt "kept the even tenor of his way," secure in the confidence and good opinion of the King, his master, and towering above all his fellows. During these ten years he was also largely in advance of his era, an enlightened advocate of solid and substantial progress, and a supporter of almost every social and political improvement which since his time has been practically carried out.

But from and after this date the circumstances and surroundings are so changed that Mr. Pitt is no longer the same man that he was before. Thrown henceforth almost wholly into the arms of the King, we see him gradually taking up a retrograde position, not easily reconcilable with that forward attitude which he has hitherto occupied.

This is not the place for a history of the first French Revolution; but we may say here that those in this island who read the daily and weekly newspapers at the time, might well have started back at the horrors and atrocities of the Reign of Terror, which has made the name of Robespierre infamous for all future ages. The neck of Louis XVI. fell under the guillotine on the 21st of January, and the event, as soon as it was known in England, caused a thrill of horror through the country. On the 1st of February, Mr. Pitt, in his place in the House of Commons, denounced it as "the foulest and most atrocious deed which the world had yet had occasion to attest." His course towards the French people received the cordial support of by far the greater part of the Opposition in both Houses ; and new penalties were imposed on those who should hold any traitorous correspondence with the enemy. But by far the larger part of the Continental powers held selfishly aloof from action against the new Republic, and so the brunt of the war fell on England, and on Austria, whom Mr. Pitt found it necessary to support by large subsidies. The armies sent into the field by the French Republic proved formidable troops, and for many months they not only held the armies of our allies at bay, but gained several victories over them, while they had also to contend against Royalist uprisings in the south of France and in La Vendée. At sea, however, our admirals asserted our superiority, and, thanks to Lords Howe, Hood, Nelson, and St. Vincent, the French ships of war were sunk or captured.

Meantime, at Edinburgh, Perth, Dundee, and other populous places in the north, seditious pamphlets were published, and meetings held, and a Convention inaugurated, which expressed a more or less complete sympathy with the "citizen" French. Trees of liberty were also planted, while the name of Pitt was devoted to public execration, as it had long been on the other side of the Channel. Such being the case, a number of informations were laid against the leaders of disaffection, and several persons of education and influence were put on their trial, with varying results. Some few were sentenced to transportation, and some were acquitted. In consequence of the report of a Committee of Secrecy, to inquire into the existence of treasonable practices, Mr. Pitt brought in a Bill for the suspension of the Habeas Corpus Act, which was passed rapidly, and with scarcely any opposition, through both Houses of Parliament.

The Duke of, Portland, who had long been looked up to as the acknowledged head of the old Whig party, now (July, 1794) formally came over to Mr. Pitt's standard, and soon after was appointed one of the Secretaries of State, and nominated a Knight of the Garter. He was followed by Lord Spencer, Mr. Windham, Mr. Thomas Grenville, and other persons of weight and character, who together brought a valuable support to the Minister engaged in an arduous and difficult war. The Duke of Portland became Secretary for the Home Department, Earl Spencer Lord Privy Seal, Earl Fitzwilliam Lord President, and Mr. Windham Secretary for War.

"To Mr. Pitt," writes Lord Stanhope,[1] "these new allies—the Duke of Portland, Lord Spencer, and Mr. Windham—were of high importance. They rallied around his standard one, and that the larger, share of the Whig party. They gave him fresh strength to resist the advance of the Re-

[1] "Life of Pitt," vol. ii. p. 53.

publican arms abroad and of the Republican doctrines at home. They gave him also, in some cases, the accession of considerable talents."

The summer also was marked by some riots in London, at Banbury, and in other places, and the abortive trials of Thomas Hardy and John Horne Tooke for high treason.

CHAPTER XVI.

WE now come to an episode in Mr. Pitt's public life which demands a few words of prefatory explanation. The government of Ireland had been for centuries a standing reproach to this country, and no one felt and knew this better than Mr. Pitt, who, here at least, was " of no party," and who exercised his judgment on all measures quite independently. He knew that the aspirations of the Irish after freedom and self-rule were of very old standing, and that no measure was so unpopular in Ireland as a proposal to form a legislative union between that kingdom and Great Britain. He could not well have forgotten—for his father would naturally have told him as a boy—how, in the very year of his birth, a rumour that such a measure was in contemplation had raised a tumult, and almost a rebellion, in the sister island.[1]　It is not therefore too much to say of him, with Lord Macaulay,

[1] " Numbers of persons in Ireland, having taken it into their heads that an Union was intended between England and Ireland, that they were to have no more (Irish) Parliaments, and were to be subject to the same taxes (with England), a mob of some thousands assembled in Dublin, broke into the House of Lords, insulted them, would have burnt the journals if they could have found them, and seated an old woman on the throne. Not content with this, they obliged all the members of both Houses that they met in the streets to take an oath that they would never consent to such an Union, or give any vote contrary to the true interest of Ireland. Many coaches of obnoxious persons were cut or broken ; one gentleman in particular narrowly escaped being hanged, a gallows being erected for that purpose. The horse and foot were drawn out on this occasion, but could not disperse the people till night."—*Annual Register*, vol. 1759, p. 129.

that he was "the first English minister who formed great designs for the benefit of Ireland."

At the close of this year (1794) the hopes of the Irish nation, or at all events of those who represented it, were raised to the highest pitch by the appointment of Earl Fitzwilliam to the vice-royalty of that kingdom. He was known to be a man of high personal character and the strictest integrity; and when he reached the shores of Ireland, carrying in his hand the olive-branch of peace, the effect was magical. Hope drove away despair, which then, as in our own time, was the parent of crime and outrage; the name of Great Britain was received with blessings instead of curses; and supplies were voted by the Irish Parliament with a cheerfulness and alacrity unknown before. But in the midst of this general rejoicing, the obstinate and bigoted old King was "at his old tricks again," and forced his too complaisant Prime Minister to recall Lord Fitzwilliam. "The cup of joy" (to use the words of the Duke of Norfolk in the House of Lords) "is suddenly dashed from their lips, and the bitterness of complaint succeeds in its place. We may be beaten," he added, " at sea, and our loss may be repaired; we may be repulsed by land, and yet recover our ground; but a gash once made in the union of two sister kingdoms may open a breach to ruin and separation." Fresh outrages, which rose almost to the verge of a rebellion, ensued; the act of the minister was severely censured by several members of the British House of Peers, though he was supported by a large majority; and in the Irish Parliament there were loud threats of Mr. Pitt himself being impeached. Lord Westmoreland, however, who had been sent over to Dublin to supersede Lord Fitzwilliam, declared that the continuance of his predecessor in office would have resulted in the "complete emancipation" of the Irish Roman Catholics, and that this would have been a "breach of the coronation oath." In the end Mr. Pitt found the two Houses of Parliament at Westminster sufficiently obsequious to whitewash his action, if they could not justify it; and the

Catholics of Ireland were forced, as they had done many times before, to "grin and bear it." Redress for their wrongs was not to come for five-and-thirty more long years of weary waiting.

On this subject a side-light is thrown by Dean Pellew in his " Life of Lord Sidmouth." He tells us that although the vice-royalty of Ireland had been promised by Mr. Pitt to Lord Camden, yet circumstances had arisen which made it necessary to appoint Lord Fitzwilliam instead, in the December of this year; but that the latter held that office for only three months, when he was recalled for "having acted quite independently of the Government, and having proceeded without their authority to carry out that *vexata quæstio*, Catholic Emancipation, then first beginning to be agitated;" and when Mr. Addington expressed a fear lest the minister's new allies should embarrass him in the Cabinet, Mr. Pitt confidently replied that "he relied much on them, but more on himself."[1]

[1] Lord Sidmouth's " Life," vol. ii. p.146.

In the Irish House of Commons, Sir Lawrence Parsons moved an address to Lord Fitzwilliam urging him not to withdraw from Ireland, and Mr. Duquerry, in seconding it, used some very strong language. He spoke of "the general despondency which this rumour had diffused through the public mind, and declared, that although in some points he had differed from gentlemen in confidence, as in the measure of the war, which he thought ruinous, and that of some taxes, on which a difference of opinion existed, yet he heartily concurred in the great measures of Administration, which were so highly beneficial to the country, and which he feared were lost for ever! Catholic Emancipation and Parliamentary Reform were gone—effectual retrenchment, a responsible Treasury Board, were both lost; and the Catholics, who, under the government of a Fitzwilliam, blended with the virtues of a Grattan, had hopes of complete emancipation, might now have the castle doors shut in their faces. The conduct of Mr. Pitt he fervently reprobated. This was no time for duplicity and backstairs influence. The situation of the country did not warrant him in raising up the hopes of the Catholics, in order to defeat them ; it was a conduct for which he deserved impeachment. He himself had a former day spoke of impeaching him, and insignificant as he was, he might do it. He felt himself the independent representative of an injured people ; he felt himself insulted by this conduct, and he called upon the House to declare the same feeling."

The forced removal of Lord Fitzwilliam from the vice-royalty of Ireland caused much bitterness and recrimination in both the British and the Irish Parliaments ; but so strong was the support offered by the landed interest in both islands to Mr. Pitt and his Ministry, that they not only escaped censure, though threatened with impeachment, but were able to command large majorities. The King was especially rejoiced at being freed from all temptation to break his coronation oath,—for so he regarded the granting of Roman Catholic Emancipation,—and the old hostile feelings of the Protestants against their unfortunate fellow-subjects were revived. But the events of the war which was raging in France drew off the attention of the people from all domestic questions; the subjects of Parliamentary Reform and of the Emancipation of the Catholics were adjourned to a more convenient season—a season which did not arrive for over a quarter of a century.

At the beginning of the year 1795 the state of affairs was critical in the extreme, in consequence of the war against France, which thus far had not proved very successful, and a large minority of the citizens of Great Britain were strongly in favour of peace, which indeed was supported by Fox and Mr. (afterwards Earl) Grey.

Mr. Pitt, however, persisted in those warlike preparations which were dictated by the King, and the enrolment of soldiers proceeded merrily on the whole, though for recruiting the wants of the navy the services of the press-gang were not found sufficient.

Accordingly, as soon as Parliament had

met (Feb. 2nd), Mr. Pitt moved, amid loud cheers, "that the House should resolve itself into a committee of the whole House, in order to consider the most effectual means of manning the navy." To this end he proposed firstly to draw for the navy one man out of every seven employed in the commercial marine ; secondly, to call upon those engaged in the inland navigation of the kingdom ; and thirdly, to authorize the magistrates to take up idle and disorderly persons, and to make them serviceable to the country.

It was suggested by one or two members that "the pensioned men of the country" (who then were to be counted by scores) should be called on to contribute their quota, while another suggested that nearly 10,000 men could be raised by employing livery servants as landsmen in the service ; and so general was the enthusiasm that Bills founded on the above resolutions were brought in and carried with scarcely a dissentient voice. Wilberforce writes in his diary under date October, 1795 :—

"Pitt appears to me to have been more

able than ever since the meeting of Parliament, and I have little doubt of his making a peace, and of the country supporting him in it."

This summer was signalized by an attempt made under the auspices of Mr. Pitt and the Cabinet to organize a descent on the western coast of France. The descent was made, but a divided command brought divided counsels and ultimate failure—a sad disappointment in Downing Street. The country, too, was much agitated by the ill news. At the opening of Parliament in the following October, the King was greeted with cries of " peace," " bread," " no war," " no Pitt;" a bullet fired from an air-gun broke one of the windows of the royal carriage, and the treatment was repeated on the return of His Majesty to St. James's Palace.

Mr. Pitt, in order to quiet the agitation, during the autumn proposed various measures to cheapen bread, and to make the supply more available to the nation at large, by mixing it with inferior grain and potatoes, prohibiting the exportation of corn, and not only allowing duty free the import of various kinds of food, but granting a bounty of twenty shillings on each quarter of wheat. At the same time he brought forward a Bill for the suppression of seditious meetings, and another for so extending the law of treason as to include all persons who should " stir up the people to hatred of His Majesty's person and of the established government and constitution." In spite of the opposition of Fox, Erskine, Lord Stanhope, the Duke of Bedford, and Lords Lauderdale and Thurlow, these were carried by large majorities. Mr. Pitt's Budget, brought forward in December, proposed a second loan of £18,000,000, and several new taxes, including one upon legacies, whether of money or of lands ;[1] and he brought down to the House a royal message expressing an "earnest

[1] The tax on legacies in money was carried, but that on land met with such opposition from the House of Commons that Mr. Pitt withdrew it ; this inequality of the law, as Lord Stanhope remarks, was not redressed till the Budget of Mr. Gladstone in 1853.

desire to conclude a treaty for a general peace, whenever it can be effected on just terms," though it was known that secretly the King was strongly in favour of the war being still carried on, to replace the Bourbons on the throne of France.

It has already been stated that Mr. Pitt was one of the most sanguine of men. But though he might look hopefully to the prospects of the foreign conflict—expecting to awe France into peace by the magnitude of his preparations—he viewed in truth the internal state of England at this time with deep anxiety. "It was his opinion," writes Lord Stanhope, "that unless a strong arm was extended, the people might be hurried by a temporary frenzy to excesses not unlike those of France. Only a few weeks from this time, as he was supping at his own house in company with two close friends—Lord Mornington and Wilberforce—he let fall this expression: 'My head would be off in six months were I to resign.'" In spite, however, of all the dangers and difficulties at home and abroad, so sanguine was Mr. Pitt at this time, that in writing to his friend Addington, the Speaker, under date October, 1795, he expresses a confident hope that if his Budget shall go off well on the meeting of Parliament, "it will give us a peace before Easter!"

In the early part of this year overtures for peace were made to the French Directory, but they met with no response ; and Fox moved (May 10th) an address to the Crown, condemning the further continuance of the war. This was negatived, though Pitt in his heart of hearts was most anxious for an end of hostilities.

In May the Parliament was dissolved ; the constituencies, as a rule, returned members who supported the Ministry ; and the harvest being above the average, Mr. Pitt's popularity was unimpaired, though he was forced to contribute to Austria a subsidy of £1,200,000 to help her to carry on the war against France. It is worthy of note that this summer witnessed the first successes of Napoleon Buonaparte against the Austrians in Northern Italy ; but an account of these

scarcely belongs to the biography of an
English statesman. In spite of Pitt's
strong remonstrance, the King of Prussia
seceded from the war, and made peace
with France. In fact, as Lord Stanhope
observes, "it was only from beyond the
bounds of Europe that good tidings
came."

Our fleet having gained some important
successes and conquests in the West Indies,
Mr. Pitt now proposed to help on the
cause of peace by offering to restore
these to France on condition of France
giving back the Low Countries to the
Emperor of Austria. But when Lord
Malmesbury arrived at Paris to carry out
this arrangement, he found the French
already active in preparing to make a
hostile descent on the coast of Ireland,
having been encouraged to do so by Wolfe
Tone. Pitt proposed a levy of 15,000 men
for the navy and army, and the raising of a
supplementary body of militia ; and in spite
of the opposition of Fox, the levies were
granted. But as a large sum was necessary for the war, he proposed, instead of

raising it in the ordinary way, to appeal to the public spirit of the nation. His wisdom was justified by the event ; he was successful even beyond his expectations, and even many of his opponents subscribed towards the "Loyalty Loan" as it was styled. This Loyalty Loan of eighteen millions was subscribed for in less than sixteen hours, the Dukes of Bridgwater and Bedford each putting his name down for £100,000. At the same time he was obliged to lay on new taxes to provide for its interest, and for the operation of the Sinking Fund ; and this he did with a sanguine spirit, and in full confidence as to the ultimate result. The new taxes which he proposed were laid on the finest kinds of tea, on auction sales, on British and foreign spirits, on sugar, on houses, on stage-coaches and on postage. At the same time he announced the subsidy which he had given to Austria at his own risk, and obtained an indemnity for that step, and also a regular grant of a further subsidy of £500,000.

To this year belongs one little episode which slightly interrupts this narrative—

that of Mr. Pitt's attachment to the Honourable Eleanor Eden, the eldest daughter of his friend Lord Auckland, a lady whom he constantly met when he went over from Holwood to Beckenham as a guest. The strong attachment—for such on Pitt's side at least it certainly was—did not proceed to a proposal or a marriage. Mr. Pitt, it is clear, admired the lady much, as much as it was in his nature to admire any one ; but he was prevented from making an offer of marriage by motives of a business character. Holwood was deeply mortgaged, and his debts besides were very large ; but, although Lord Auckland was quite willing that his daughter should run the risks of being left but poorly provided for in case of Pitt's death, Mr. Pitt thought it best to go no further. So ended this love passage, " the only one," writes Lord Stanhope, " as I believe, in the life of Pitt, without any breach of friendship on either side." It may be interesting to record here the fact that the lady, who was eighteen years Pitt's junior, married two years later Lord Hobart, who in 1804 became Earl of

Buckinghamshire, became a widow in 1816, and died childless in 1851.

We have said that Mr. Pitt was generally far-sighted, and in favour of progress and improvement. An example of his pre-science is to be found in the year 1796, when he and his Admiralty Board had submitted to their inspection a novel invention of Lord Stanhope, in the shape of a war vessel worked by steam. No doubt the invention was crude ; but, while it was rejected as useless by the Board, the idea approved itself to Mr. Pitt, who, Lord Stanhope tells us, "when consulted, urged the trial of the scheme from his own impression of its possible merits." Lord Stanhope infers from this fact that Mr. Pitt was the first person in high office who discerned, however dimly in the distance, the future importance of steam to navigation, and who really desired to put it to the test, and this, too, at a time when "his own First Lord of the Admiralty looked down upon the project as an empty dream."

On many other subjects Mr. Pitt was far in advance of his age. In one of the debates on the relief of the poor in rural districts, he said :—

" I should wish that an opportunity were given of restoring the original purity of the Poor Laws, and of removing those corruptions by which they have been obscured. . . . These great points of granting relief according to the number of children, preventing removals at the caprice of the parish officer, and of making them subscribe to friendly societies, would tend in a very great degree to remove every ground of complaint. . . . All this, however, I will . confess is not enough, if we do not engraft upon it resolutions to discourage relief where it is not wanted. . . . The extension of schools of industry is also an object of material importance. The suggestion of these schools was originally drawn from Lord Hale and Mr. Locke, and on such authority I have no hesitation in recommending the plan to the encouragement of the Legislature. . . . Such a plan would convert the relief granted to the poor into an encouragement of industry, instead of being, as it is by the present

Poor Laws, a premium for idleness and a school for sloth. The law which prohibits giving relief where any visible property remains should be abolished. That degrading condition should be withdrawn. No temporary occasion should force a British subject to part with the last shilling of his little capital, and to descend to a state of wretchedness from which he never could recover, merely that he might be entitled to a casual supply."

CHAPTER XVII.

THE winter of 1796–7 was remarkable for two abortive landings of French crews, at Bantry Bay, in Ireland, and at Fishguard, on the coast of Pembrokeshire; but in both cases the invaders were repelled almost without bloodshed. These enterprises, however, were only intended as preludes to an invasion of Great Britain on a larger scale. With this object in view, the French Directory proposed a concerted invasion of their own, the Spanish, and the Dutch fleets ; but before the three fleets could meet, Sir John Jervis engaged the Spaniards off Cape St. Vincent, and, aided by Collingwood and Nelson, gained a splendid victory, for which he was raised to the peerage as Lord St. Vincent.

In spite of this great victory, however, a very dark day was at hand for England. Consequent on the large export of bullion in subsidies and loans to foreign Powers, the funds in store at the Bank were at so low an ebb that, by an order of the Privy Council, the Bank of England was prohibited from issuing any cash, the merchants and bankers of the city at the same time agreeing to receive and to tender bank-notes only. This saved the public credit, and so the country was rescued in spite of the ill-omened bodings of Fox and his friends. This temporary suspension of cash payments gave rise to many epigrams, amongst which, perhaps, this was the wittiest and the best, paraphrased

from a note in " The Pursuits of Literature " :—

> " Of Augustus and Rome
>   The poets still warble,
> How he found it of brick
> And left it of marble.
>
> So of Pitt and of England
>   Men may say without vapour,
> That he found it of gold
> And left it of paper."

In a few weeks followed another event
which caused almost equal alarm—a mutiny
in our fleet at Spithead. The demands
of the men for increased pay and other
advantages were seen to be founded on
reason and fairness; and, chiefly by the
instrumentality of Lords Bridport and
Howe, the crews returned to their allegiance, every point which they claimed being
conceded, and this without a drop of
bloodshed. A similar mutiny was commenced at the Nore, but it also was quelled
by the firmness of the Government and
the officers, Parker and one or two of the
ringleaders only being hung at the yard-
arm. Had this mutiny broken out into

open rebellion, it is more than probable that the sun of England would have set in reality, as has been so often prophesied that it will some day.

The summer of this year was marked by the death of one of Pitt's personal friends, and one who under other circumstances might have proved one of his trusted colleagues—Edmund Burke, on whom he had been able to persuade the King to settle a pension a year or two before, when, broken-hearted at the death of his only son, he withdrew from public life.

In this year we find another instance of Pitt's superiority to the prejudices of the vulgar herd; for he supported Mr. Wilberforce's motion to allow Roman Catholics to serve in the militia, and was for a time, in consequence, estranged from his old friend, Lord Grenville, who caused the Bill to be thrown out by the Lords.

In the course of the session, Pitt represented to the King "the gradual and increasing difficulties of finance," and told him of the unanimous opinion of his Cabinet that the first favourable opportunity should be taken for negotiating with France for peace ; the King, for a wonder, acquiesced ; and early in July Lord Malmesbury was sent to Lille to agree on terms, but after a month or two spent in fruitless discussions, the negotiations were broken off, and Lord Malmesbury returned to London, *re infectâ*, to the great disappointment of both countries. In fact, if the truth must be told, while the King was obstinately in favour of continuing the war, his Prime Minister, on the contrary, scarcely ever abandoned the hope of a peace being made, even though he knew that he had the doubtful honour of having a price set upon his head at Paris.

In the September of this year, Mr. Pitt received a great shock from the death of his near relative, Mr. Edward Eliot ; "his grief," Mr. G. Rose wrote, "on this occasion exceeded all conception." He spent the autumn at Walmer, amusing his leisure hours by occasional translations from Horace's odes into English verse.

During this autumn the French and

Dutch, urged on by Wolfe Tone and other restless spirits, fitted out another fleet in order to operate in combination against England, but they were defeated (Oct. 11th) at the Battle of Camperdown.

When Parliament reassembled in November, after the Vacation, Mr. Pitt produced his Budget, which revealed the fact that a deficit of nineteen millions had to be provided for. The minister proposed to cover this void in part by a new loan of twelve millions, and partly by augmenting the assessed taxes to three times, and prospectively to four times, their existing amount. Such a heavy impost called out the strenuous opposition of Fox and Sheridan, to whom now were added George Tierney and Sir Francis Burdett; but, in spite of much popular excitement out of doors, the minister was able to carry his measure by a large majority. On the 19th of December, however, when accompanying the King to a special service of thanksgiving in St. Paul's for the recent victories of Lords Howe, St. Vincent, and Duncan, over the French, the Spaniards, and the Dutch, Mr. Pitt was hooted and insulted by the mob, and his carriage was escorted home in safety only by a troop of the London Light Horse.[1]

It is worthy of note that in the month of November in this year, Pitt's friends, headed by George Canning and George Ellis, started the *Anti-Jacobin*, a witty periodical which helped for some years to cast ridicule on the utopian dreams of French philosophers and those revolutionary spirits at home who, for the want of a better name, were known as "Jacobins." The publication elicited several counter-attacks, one of which, "An Epistle to the Editor of the *Anti-Jacobin*," was written by the Hon. William Lamb, afterwards Lord Melbourne, and First Lord of the Treasury.

In January, the "Friends of the People" and his other admirers gave a public dinner to Fox, at the Crown and Anchor, in the Strand, when the Duke of Norfolk proposed as a toast, "The Sove-

[1] Annual Register, 1797, p. 80.

reignty of the People," for which he was dismissed from his Lord Lieutenancy of the West Riding of Yorkshire. This spurred the dormant spirit of Pitt's supporters, who, at the suggestion of Henry Addington, then Speaker of the House of Commons, came forward to aid the State with voluntary contributions from their private purses. Several public bodies and City Companies also sent in voluntary contributions; the City of London subscribed £10,000, and the Bank of England no less than £200,000. "On the whole," writes Lord Stanhope, "these free-will offerings, exclusive of £300,000 which subsequently came from India, amounted to two millions sterling."

In spite of this timely subvention, Mr. Pitt found it necessary to raise further supplies. This he proposed to do by a partial commutation of the Land Tax, which was to be made perpetual, its proceeds being applied to the reduction of the National Debt. Thus he hoped that the public revenue would be assisted, and also a new impulse be given to the public credit.   In spite of the obvious unfairness of its provisions, no new assessment having been made for a century, during which the value of many localities had been largely altered, the Bill was carried by large majorities.

Even while this Bill was in progress, further necessities arose to the extent of three millions, which called in April for a second or supplementary Budget. A new loan for that amount was accordingly proposed, and to provide for the interest on it there must be a further tax on armorial bearings and on the finer kinds of tea. There was no alternative but to submit, and these were also carried.

The great need of further supplies arose largely from the disturbed condition of Ireland, where a portion of the people were in touch with the French semi-Jacobins, urged by Wolfe Tone and other exiles to do all in their power to annoy and hamper Mr. Pitt's administration. Ill-blood also had risen between the Protestants of Ulster, who now began to call themselves "Orangemen" (after William

III.), and their poorer and less educated Roman Catholic brethren. Instead of endeavouring to pacify Ireland by remedial measures, the authorities of Dublin Castle resolved on coercive measures, and carried them out in spite of all the eloquence of Henry Grattan. It was refused, in spite of the troubles in France, to allow Roman Catholics to sit and vote in the Irish House of Parliament ; and Grattan retired from public life in despair of justice or tranquillity. The Rebellion of '98 quickly followed.

The story of the Rebellion of '98 has been often told, and need not be repeated here in any detail. After a few weeks of desultory warfare, it was put down by the forces of the Crown, and a few of the leading rebels were executed ; but Lord Cornwallis, to his credit, tempered justice with mercy.

This, however, did not prevent the leaders of the Irish party from keeping their eyes steadily fixed on the offing, in the hope that they would soon discern the arrival of assistance in the shape of ships and stores. Nor did they look in vain, though the aid sent was insignificant, the greater part of the French fleet being about to be despatched to Egypt to carry out the ideas and dreams of Napoleon. On August 22nd, three French frigates and some transports which had been despatched from La Rochelle under General Humbert, landed at Killala, in the county of Mayo. They were subsequently reinforced by a further force of nine frigates and three thousand troops, but these were defeated by Sir John Borlase Warren, and only two of the frigates escaped back to France. Wolfe Tone, who had accompanied the invading force, and a few others also, were condemned to death; but Tone anticipated death by suicide.

This abortive rising in Ireland had in itself the seeds of results which, whether for good as some think, or for evil as others assert most positively, have influenced the history of Ireland for the best part of a century; and, at all events, formed a pretext for saddling a " Legislative Union " on a reluctant nation.

From the very commencement of the Irish difficulties, Mr. Pitt had decided to bring forward an entirely new and comprehensive Act of Union which, he hoped, would result in uniting the two nations into one harmonious whole. He knew that to quell the insurrection by force of arms was not the only part of his duty, and that to return to the old system would be at once ill-advised and dangerous. How far the Union justified, or failed to justify, the hopes of those who planned and introduced it, will be seen hereafter.

On Friday, May 25th, when Pitt brought in a Bill for the more effectual manning of the navy, a misunderstanding arose between himself and Mr. George Tierney, which led to what was in those days styled a hostile encounter, but in common speech is known as a duel. A challenge sent by Mr. Tierney next day forced Mr. Pitt to "give him satisfaction."

The duel was fought on Putney Heath, on Sunday, May 27th, 1798. The latter had sent a challenge to the minister, in consequence of some angry words in the

House of Commons. Pitt was attended by Mr. Dudley Ryder (afterwards Lord Harrowby), and Mr. Tierney by Mr. George Walpole. Standing at twelve paces, each fired at the same moment, but without effect. The second fire was attended with the same result, when the seconds interfered, and declared that sufficient satisfaction had been given. Lord Holland thus writes of the duel in his " Memoirs of the Whig Party " :—

"Mr. Pitt's irritability to Mr. Tierney was very near involving fatal consequences. Mr. Tierney, I have been told, annexed to Mr. Pitt's words a meaning which they were not meant to convey ; but the latter's imperious manner in refusing all explanations when called on . . . made it difficult for Mr. Tierney not to resent his language. The circumstances of the duel are well known. It was fought on a Sunday—a circumstance which gave a handle to much vulgar abuse against Mr. Pitt. He did indeed urge the necessity of fighting immediately, if at all, because it was not proper for one in his situation to maintain any protracted correspondence on such a subject.

"They fought near a gibbet on which the body of the malefactor Abershaw was yet suspended. . . . Mr. Tierney's second, General Walpole, leaped over the furze bushes for joy when Mr. Pitt fired in the air. Some time elapsed, and some discussion between the seconds took place before the affair was finally and amicably adjusted. Mr. Pitt very consistently insisted on one condition, which was in itself reasonable : that he was not to quit the ground without the whole matter being completely terminated. The danger of Mr. Tierney had indeed been great. Had Mr. Pitt fallen, the fury of the times would probably have condemned him to exile or death, without reference to the provocation which he had received, and the sanction which custom had given to the redress which he sought."

In the early autumn of this year, an abundant harvest, a flourishing exchequer, the suppression of the Irish Rebellion, and, above all, Nelson's surprising victory at the mouth of the Nile, had not only restored Mr. Pitt to his wonted vigour and confidence, but had also suggested to his mind the idea of another Continental war. This he thought the best means to ensure a permanent peace.

About the middle of November the outline of the Union proposed by Mr. Pitt was sent to Dublin to be submitted to the Irish Parliament. The Bill in its crude state imposed no entire disfranchisement on any county or borough, but only such a reduction in the number of members as should limit them to a hundred in all, and at the same time there was no limit fixed to the creation of new Irish peerages by the Crown. The Bill was to be considered as soon as the Irish Houses should meet in the following January.

In December, on the meeting of Parliament at Westminster, Mr. Pitt laid before the House his plan of a new Income Tax, which he imposed on all persons having £65 a year, and rising by a graduated scale up to the owners of £200 a year, upon which, and on all incomes of a higher amount, ten

per cent. was to be paid, and no distinction
was made between incomes derived from
land or from the funds and those made by
men in professions. The Bill was carried
by large majorities in the House of Commons, and without a division in the Lords,
and it professed to be only a temporary
tax, to be withdrawn as soon as peace
should return. In addition to paying this
tax, many persons in high places set an
example of helping the Government by
voluntary aids, Mr. Pitt and the Speaker,
Mr. Addington, each promising £2,000
annually, while the King gave a third of
his Privy Purse, or £20,000 a year.

CHAPTER XVIII.

WE must now return to the subject of the projected Union between Great Britain and Ireland.

It was in vain that the opponents of the proposed Union pointed out to the British House of Commons, among other arguments, that the measure would encourage absenteeism by taking off to Westminster those noblemen and country gentlemen who lived then for half the year in Dublin, and so tend to drain the sister island of money. In vain did Fox, Sheridan, and Grey raise their voices against the injustice of forcing such an arrangement upon Ireland against the will of her people at large, and declare that the voice of that people ought to be first ascertained and declared by an appeal to the hustings at a General Election. Mr. Pitt had the ear of the King; he commanded a strong and subservient majority in the House of Commons at Westminster; he had but to bribe the upper classes of Ireland by scattering amongst them a profusion of new coronets and promotions in the ranks of the Irish peerage, and to pay out of the pockets of British taxpayers some £750,000 to the owners of "pocket boroughs" in Ireland, and he knew that "the game was in his hands."

It is asserted by Pitt's friends, and probably the assertion is true, that he always intended the boon of the Union to be accompanied, or at all events speedily followed, by the boon of Roman Catholic Emancipation. Probably the minister was sincere in this intention ; but he reckoned without his host when he calculated his power with the bigoted monarch ; and the consequence was that only one-half of the boon was conceded—the bread was given to the Irish without the butter which ought to have accompanied it, and the crust in consequence tasted dry and savourless, and was therefore accepted reluctantly and without thanks.   In Ireland the measure evoked no cheers of joy or of gratitude; not a bonfire blazed in honour of its passing into law.   It was with many a sigh and many a tear that the members of the Irish Legislature saw the doors of the Parliament House at Dublin closed, the building itself turned to other purposes, and the Chair and the Sergeant's mace carried off to the private home of the last Irish Speaker, Sir John Foster.

It is not too much to say that Mr. Pitt and his friends had recourse to wholesale bribery in order to make the proposed Union palatable to the Irish.   Peerages and other honours were showered in profusion on those who were loudest in their opposition at first, but who afterwards became as docile as lambs. Those who held sinecure posts or paid employments, and who held out against the measure, were dismissed and superseded. In the event, a proposal to maintain the " independent Legislature as established in Ireland in 1782 " was defeated by a single vote.

The question, therefore, was allowed to sleep for a time, and further bribery and intimidation were employed to bring round the dissentients. The only excuse that can be urged on behalf of such means must be the fact that Mr. Pitt thought the end not only justifiable, but necessary for the preservation of the Constitution.

There can be no doubt also that the fact that the proposed Union, though rejected at Dublin, was accepted and carried at Westminster, was largely owing to Mr. Pitt's eloquence, which never rose to a higher pitch than it did in the speech in which he urged its acceptance. In it he urged strongly the possibility of the two rival Parliaments coming to conflicting decisions about such burning questions as the war against France, or the terms of a regency, as proving its necessity.

Lord Stanhope tells us that this speech (Jan. 31st, 1799) was the only one, except that on the proposed Sinking Fund (Feb. 17th, 1792), and that on the overtures from France (Jan. 22nd, 1800), which Mr. Pitt ever took the trouble to revise for the press.

It was in vain that Sheridan moved an amendment to the usual address, "entreating His Majesty not to listen to the counsels of those who should advise an union of the legislatures of the two kingdoms under the existing circumstances of the Empire." Pitt was backed by so overwhelming a majority of the country gentlemen, that the amendment was negatived without a division (Jan. 23rd), and only a week later (Jan. 31st) Pitt moved eight resolutions echoing back the royal advice, and by a majority of 140 to 15 the House went into committee on the measure.

The resolutions may be shortly stated as follows :—

"In order to promote and secure the

essential interests of Great Britain and
Ireland, and to consolidate the strength
and resources of the Empire, it is advis-
able to unite the two kingdoms into one,
in such manner and on such terms as may
be established by acts of the respective
Parliaments of the said kingdoms.   In the
first place, Great Britain and Ireland are
to be united into one kingdom, by the
name of ' The United Kingdom of Great
Britain and Ireland,' and the succession to
the monarchy of the united kingdoms shall
be settled in the same manner as the
imperial crown of the said kingdoms of
Great Britain and Ireland now stands
limited and settled.   The said United
Kingdom to be represented in one and the
same Parliament, and such a number of
lords spiritual and temporal, and such a
number of members of the House of Commons as shall be hereafter agreed upon by
acts of the respective Parliaments, as afore-
said, shall sit and vote in the said Parliament on the part of Ireland, and shall be
returned in such manner as shall be fixed
by an act of the Parliament of Ireland

previous to the union. And every member of the said Parliament of the United Kingdom shall take and subscribe the same oaths, and make the same declaration as the law requires of the members of the Parliaments of Great Britain and Ireland. The Churches of England and Ireland, and the doctrine, worship, and government thereof, to be preserved as now by law established. His Majesty's subjects in Ireland shall at all times hereafter be entitled to the same privileges in respect of trade and navigation in all ports and places belonging to Great Britain, and in all cases where treaties shall be made by the Sovereign with any foreign Power. No duty shall be imposed on the import or export between Great Britain and Ireland of any articles now free of duty, and on other articles there shall be a moderate rate of equal duties, such rate to be approved by the respective Parliaments previous to the union, and to be liable, after a certain time, to be diminished, but in no case to be increased. Goods which may at any time hereafter be imported into Great Britain, shall be importable through either kingdom into the other subject to the like duties and regulations as if the same were imported directly from foreign parts. All other matters of trade and commerce, except such as may be specially agreed upon before the union, shall be regulated from time to time by the united Parliament." The resolutions further provided that the charge arising from the payment of the interest or sinking fund for the reduction of the debt incurred in either kingdom before the union should continue to be separately defrayed by Great Britain and Ireland respectively, and that for a limited number of years the future ordinary expenses of the United Kingdom, in peace or war, should be defrayed by Great Britain and Ireland jointly in the proportions established by the respective Parliaments previous to the union. The laws in force at the time of the union, and the jurisdiction of all civil or ecclesiastical courts within the respective kingdoms, were to remain as then by law established within the same, subject only to such alterations or regulations as from time to time might appear to the Parliament of the United Kingdom to be required.

From the speeches by which Pitt induced the House of Commons to consider, and in effect to approve these resolutions, it is clear that both the King and the supporters of his minister professed to have in view the security of the Empire itself. The excesses of the French Revolution, and the " Jacobinism " which had spread into England, were exercising on the people an influence which could not be ignored ; and the fact that an attempt had been twice made by a French fleet to land on the coast of Ireland, in the hope of detaching the sister island from the British throne, was largely at the bottom of the measure proposed as a remedy. All sorts of excuses, however, were made by Pitt for pressing forward this measure, such as commercial jealousies between two countries, and the danger—a speculative rather than a practical one, it must be owned—of those Legislatures acting in opposition to each other. For instance, on the question of the appointment of a Regency, the Irish Legislature might differ from that of Great Britain in selecting a Regent, or they might agree in their choice, but choose the Regent on a different principle. It was urged by Pitt that the settlement of 1782 was not really a final adjustment, but "one that left the connection between Great Britain and Ireland exposed to all the attacks of party, and all the effects of accident." He also urged the existence of "internal treason," imported from France into Ireland, as a further reason for fixing the connection (between England and Ireland) "on a more solid basis." In spite of the strong opposition of the Irish House of Commons, Pitt insisted on the measure on "demonstrable grounds of utility," as "calculated to add to the strength and power of the Empire," and urged that it was supported by a large part of the manufacturing and commercial interest in the sister island.

On learning for the first time, towards the close of January, that Mr. Pitt intended to follow up his measure for the Union with Ireland by a supplemental gift of Roman Catholic Emancipation, and finding that he would be expected to announce this on opening Parliament on the 2nd of February, the King took fright, declaring that he was about to be made to violate his coronation oath. "Were he to grant this," he told the Duke of Portland, "he should betray his trust, and forfeit his crown;" and it was the Duke's opinion that, rather than yield to the demands of his minister, he would have gone to the block. He was also much distressed at the great pains which Pitt had taken to keep back from him this intention till the last moment. "The measure had taken him by surprise, and had hurt him much."[1] Accordingly, on the 29th of January the King wrote to Addington, urging him to use his utmost endeavours to divert his friend from his purpose. But this was beyond his power; and, on learning from Addington what the King's sentiments were, Mr. Pitt tendered his resignation to

[1] "Lord Malmesbury's Diaries," vol. iv. pp. 8, 9.

His Majesty. On the February 5th, the King accepted his resignation, with deep regret, we may be sure.

The King then, of his own accord, offered the post of Prime Minister to Mr. Addington, in whom he felt great confidence, and who had been Pitt's friend from childhood. All his difficulties in accepting the post were mastered by the generosity of Pitt, who "not only agreed with the King that it was Addington's duty to accept the Premiership, but made him the offer of his full influence and support, saying to him, 'Addington, I see nothing but ruin if you hesitate.'"[1] At the same time the King wrote to Dr. Hurd, Bishop of Worcester, stating that he has "permitted Mr. Pitt to retire from his service," on account of "an unfortunate opinion implanted in his mind that it is necessary to pass the Catholic Relief Act and to repeal the Test Act." So deeply was the King grieved at this step, that he again became seriously ill, and for some days it was on the cards that

[1] Jesse's "Memoirs of George III.," vol. iii. p. 247.

he would have a repetition of that mental disorder which prostrated him in 1788. What is more, he was conscious of the fact; and to Lord Chatham he said, with some asperity, " Whatever I have beyond a cold, I owe to your brother. What has he not to answer for, who is the cause of my having been ill at all ? "[1] So ill indeed did the King become, that some weeks elapsed before it was possible to effect the change of seals, which had been arranged. Early in March, however, he was again convalescent ; and no doubt it helped on his recovery to learn that Pitt had assured him that, whether in or out of office, he would never again agitate the question of Catholic Emancipation.[2]

The new Cabinet (March, 1801), it may be here observed by the way, included the Duke of Portland, Lord Chatham, and Lord Westmoreland, and was strengthened by the accession of Lord Hawkesbury (afterwards

---

[1] Jesse, vol. iii. pp. 253, 260.
[2] " Malmesbury's Diaries," vol. iv. p. 34 ; "Colchester's Diary," vol. i. p. 255 ; " Rose's Diary," vol. i. pp. 360, 426.

Earl of Liverpool), of Lord Hobart (afterwards Earl of Buckinghamshire), and also
of Lord Eldon, who afterwards became
Lord Chancellor.

But scarcely was Addington seated in
his chair in Downing Street, when Pitt
began to feel that, as he was now released,
or had released himself, from his engage-
ments with the Catholic party, there could
be no obstacle to his picking up again the
reins which he had let fall into Addington's
hands, if only Addington would waive his
claims. His friends, too, pressed upon him
the argument that, if he could reinstate
himself in Downing Street, he would himself stand better with the public, many of
whom blamed him for deserting the helm
at a critical moment. And certainly all
would agree that it was desirable at such a
time that the best man should steer the
ship of the State. In spite of all his
scholarship, his learning, his polished manners, and business habits, Mr. Addington
had never impressed himself on the nation
as a man of power ; in fact, his nomination
as Premier had been " received," as we learn

from Lord Malmesbury, " with derision and even slight in the Legislature," and we find Pitt himself exacting from his friend George Canning, then quite a young man, a promise not to laugh at the appointment.[1] In fact, had Addington been really wise, and seen himself as others saw him, he would have sought the King out, and said to him, " Now that the Catholic question is asleep and forgotten, I am ready to re-sign my office to Mr. Pitt." [2]

But Addington, very naturally, did not take the same view of the situation; and his native self-confidence was encouraged by a chorus of applauding relatives, who thoroughly believed in his powers, and en-tertained every hope of preferment if he held office. " Others," he said, " might, if they pleased, suggest such an arrangement to the King; but he would not be guilty of political suicide." Doubtless, a word from the King would have led him to make way for Pitt ; but the King could hardly offer such a hint to a man whom he had pressed

---

[1] " Malmesbury's Diary," vol. iv. p. 5.
[2] *Ibid.*

to accept the highest office. The King was glad of any arrangement which would give him the services of Pitt and Addington at once; and he even said to his two ministers quietly, " If we three do but keep together, all will do well."[1]

The farewell interview between Pitt and his royal master took place on the 14th of March, when the King thanked him cordially for his services, and spoke of him to both Rose and Lord Eldon in terms of the highest admiration. On the 17th of the same month, the new ministers were gazetted. Pitt had already moved and carried the Budget for the year, though no longer actually in office ; so there was less work for Addington to take in hand.

Very naturally the conduct of Mr. Pitt in resigning the Premiership at so critical a moment was severely canvassed and criticised by his friends as well as by his foes. His friends, of course, held that when a strong government was demanded, and only a weak one was in prospect, it was the

[1] Pellew's " Life of Sidmouth," vol. i. p. 331.

duty of a patriotic minister to stand by his sovereign ; while others, equally honest in their sentiments, held that it was his duty, at all cost, to see *ne quid res publica detrimenti caperet.*

On retiring from office, Pitt took a small house in Park Place, St. James's Street, which had been occupied by an Under Secretary of State ; and there he lived in comparative retirement, declining all dinners except with intimate friends, like Wilberforce, Dundas, Rose, Canning, and Long, who followed him faithfully. As a private member of Parliament, it is on record that he took his seat "on the right hand of the Speaker's chair, in the third row from the floor, and in an angle next to one of the iron pillars"; and his seat was pointed out, as long as the old House of Commons stood, with pride and reverence by his disciples.

As weeks and months went on, and Mr. Addington failed to satisfy the hopes of the country, and even of his own party, there can be no ground for wonder that Mr. Pitt began to lose more and more of his trust in the man whom the King had made his successor. Nor was it only in his confidential communications with Canning and other private friends that he was betrayed into expressing dissatisfaction at the manner in which Addington was conducting the business of the nation. For instance, while conversing with Lord Malmesbury in the month of November, we not only find him objecting to the King's speech as being "very vague and loose," but pointing to one of the statements in it, and adding that it "was false." Again, when Addington submitted to him his financial exposition, preparatory to his bringing his Budget before the House of Commons, Pitt not only animadverted on the enormity of the miscalculations—estimated by him to amount to no less a sum than £2,800,000, but on another occasion expressed his conviction that "the whole of those statements were founded on gross errors, arising from the most childish ignorance."[1]

[1] Jesse's "Memoirs of George III.," vol. iii. p. 299.

CHAPTER XIX.

*Motives of the Union—The King's Obstinacy—
Addington's Cabinet—Lord Nelson's Victory
at Copenhagen—Hostile Measures on Part of
Napoleon Buonaparte—Pitt, out of Office,
resides in Baker Street — Addington's
Budget a Failure—Cabal of Pitt's Friends
to reinstate him—Open Estrangement between
Pitt and Addington— The Public Voice demands the Restoration of Pitt to Power.*

TO return to the subject of the Union
between England and Ireland.

There can be little doubt that, however
we may regard the Union, after it became
un fait accompli, the motives in which it
originated will not bear a close inspection,
any more than will the means by which it
was matured.

Lord Cornwallis, who was from his
position compelled to carry it into

effect, said that he was "obliged to pay compliments to men whom he should like to kick." The Irish Protestants were drawn into allegiance by a lavish distribution of titles and money, while the Roman Catholics were treated with contempt and indifference. According to Lord Russell, a more "disgusting" process than the transactions connected with the Irish Union could not well be, although he allows that Pitt held out hopes to the Roman Catholics, and, better still, wished to give effect to them. Reckoning on his sixteen years' service at the head of the Government, and also on his substantial majority in both Houses of Parliament, Pitt thought that his advice to the King with the object of firmly cementing the Union would be followed, but in this hope he found himself entirely mistaken.

The obstinacy of the King thus defeated Mr. Pitt, who, if he had really believed the soundness of his own position all along in this matter, ought to have told His Majesty plainly that his credit and honour as a minister were at stake, and that if the

King would not grant the Roman Catholics that relief to which they were entitled, and which he had led them to believe would be granted, then he must cease to wear the royal livery. Had Mr. Pitt acted thus, in all probability the King would have given way, and his Prime Minister would never have been tempted to quit Downing Street. *Sed Dis aliter visum est.* Unfortunately, he hesitated and, as we have seen, gave the King an opportunity of consulting with others less far-sighted and less patriotic than himself, and who were able to play upon the King's conscientious fears about his coronation oath. When Pitt wrote tendering his resignation of the Premiership, the King was taken aback, but was obliged to accept the resignation, though before doing so he proposed as a compromise that Mr. Pitt should continue in office, he, the King, maintaining utter silence on the question of Catholic Relief, and that Mr. Pitt on his part should forbear to bring it forward. But Pitt had too much pride to acquiesce in such an arrangement.

The new Cabinet was reunited by the accession of Lord Eldon as Chancellor, in the place of Lord Loughborough, now made an Earl, and of Lord Hawkesbury (afterwards Earl of Liverpool) as Secretary for Foreign Affairs; Mr. Law (afterwards Lord Ellenborough) and Mr. Spencer Percival (subsequently Premier) becoming Attorney and Solicitor General. In the first debate which followed on the advent of the new Cabinet, Mr. Pitt somewhat haughtily vindicated himself from the charge—shrinking from difficulties—which some among his former friends and followers had brought against him. Fox naturally spoke in strong terms of censure of both the late and the new Administration; but as he found that he could gain nothing by seeking to overthrow it, and as Pitt cordially supported it—for the present—all overt and systematic opposition to Mr. Addington came to an end.

A few weeks afterwards arrived the good news that Lord Nelson had gained for the Ministry a brilliant victory over the Danish fleet at Copenhagen, by purposely shutting his eye to Sir Peter Parker's signal for "leaving off action." For this Parker was recalled, and Nelson raised to a Viscountcy. Almost at the same time (as mentioned already) the nation learnt of the victory of Abercromby over the French at Aboukir Bay, in Egypt. At the end of the session the royal speech referred to these brilliant successes by land and sea as giving hope of a restoration of peace, a hope which was increased by the prospect of an abundant harvest.

On quitting office it was found by his friends that, owing to the carelessness of Pitt for his domestic expenditure, he was in debt to the extent of more than £40,000; but still he refused the offer of a present of £30,000 out of the King's Privy Purse, and a still larger lump sum which had been voted to him by the City of London. But his personal friends raised nearly £12,000 to meet the most pressing of his liabilities; and he realized £15,000 more by the sale of his favourite home at Holwood.

The hopes of peace expressed by the Royal Speech were soon realized; for

on the 1st of October the preliminaries
were signed between England and France,
and when Parliament met on the 28th
of the same month, the King was able
to announce that peace had been made
with the northern Powers also. Mr. Pitt,
—though, to tell the truth, he had himself
had no small share in the arrangements
with France—declared his strong approval
of the conduct of the Government, and
his gratitude to them for the steps which
they had taken in the direction of peace.
Wilberforce, in his diary, on December 1st
records the fact, that, in spite of Fox and
Sheridan, opposition is "melting away
manifestly"; that "Addington goes on
well, is honest and respectable, and im-
proves in speaking"; and that "Pitt
supports most magnanimously, and assists
in every way." At Christmas he accompanied Pitt to Cambridge, where they were
entertained at a great feast in the Hall
of Trinity College; and so the first year
of the new century ended with brighter
prospects for the future, in spite of the fact
that Roman Catholic Emancipation and

the Abolition of the Slave Trade were still among the questions which were pending for solution. The former was not settled for nearly, nor the latter for more than, thirty years.

CHAPTER XX.

Pitt and Addington—Vote of Thanks to Pitt, and Public Dinner—Napoleon's Hostile Movements in the South of Europe—Conspiracy of Col. Despard—Pitt removes to Baker Street —Pitt's Friends desire his Return to Office— His Disappointment at Addington's Budget —Misunderstanding between Pitt and Addington—A Coalition Ministry suggested.

WHEN Parliament met in January, 1802, Mr Addington showed his regard for Mr. Pitt by giving seats at the Privy Council Board to his two personal friends and satellites, Mr. George Rose and Mr. Charles Long. The Speaker, Sir John Mitford, was sent to Ireland as Chancellor, being created Lord Redesdale, and was succeeded in the chair by Mr. Charles Abbott, afterwards Lord Colchester. Erskine and one or two others of the moderate Whigs made overtures of supporting the new ministers; and though Mr. Pitt was somewhat chafed at Addington saying only a few brief words in his defence, when accused by Tierney, in his absence, of laxity in his administration of the public money, yet the cloud of misunderstanding was at once removed, and the conclusion of peace at Amiens on the 27th of March sent up the funds once more and rejoiced the hearts of the people. Mr. Addington, in bringing forward his Budget, was able to propose a large remission of taxation, and to repeal the Income Tax; and we learn from Mr. N. Vansittart, afterwards Chancellor of the Exchequer, and eventually Lord Bexley, that "Mr. Pitt was consulted with respect to these arrangements, and fully approved of them all." [1]

A special vote of thanks to Mr. Pitt personally, as well as to His Majesty's ministers, was passed by the Houses of Parliament; and his birthday was celebrated by a public dinner at Merchant Tay-

---

[1] See Pellew's "Life of Sidmouth," vol. ii. p. 61.

lors' Hall, when Lord Spencer took the chair, and the new song, written for the occasion by George Canning himself,—

" Here's a health to the pilot that weathered the storm,"—

was sung with the greatest enthusiasm. The great popularity of the peace was shown by the result of the General Election, which followed in the course of the summer. The ministers commanded a large and increased majority, while several of the Opposition found great difficulty in obtaining seats.

Soon after this, at Mr. Pitt's urgent recommendation, Lord Castlereagh joined the Addington Cabinet as President of the Board of Control. Mr. Pitt spent the summer and autumn partly at Walmer and partly at Bath, and in spite of some mutual dissatisfaction, on the part of France and of England, upon various points of the treaty which had not been fully carried out—a dissatisfaction fostered on either side by an unwise press—Great Britain enjoyed the blessing of a rest from the horrors and troubles of war, at all events for a time.

The First Consul of France, however, would seem to have been resolved that it should be only for a time, as in August and September decrees of the French Senate were issued annexing the island of Elba and the territory of Piedmont. This was followed by the occupation of Parma and Placentia, and the march of an army into Switzerland, under the pretext of putting down an internal civil dissension. Under these circumstances, the more far-sighted politicians in this country began to reflect, and to ask themselves whether, if war should break out again, Addington was "the right man in the right place." According to Lord Malmesbury, great dissatisfaction on this score was expressed in many influential quarters in different parts of the kingdom ; and the general uneasiness was increased by a secret conspiracy, got up by a Colonel Despard, to assassinate the King as he went to open Parliament in November. The plot, was betrayed beforehand, and the affair never came off ;

but Colonel Despard was tried for high treason, condemned, and hanged in the following February (1803).

For a part of the time that he was out of office, during the Addington Administration (October, 1802–3), Mr. Pitt occupied the house, No. 14, York Place, a continuation northwards of Baker Street—a situation which may have been convenient in point of economy, but was sadly distant from the House of Commons. He removed to this house in October, 1802, from Park Place, but he did not occupy it long, as he was ordered to spend the latter part of the autumn at Bath, in order to drink the waters.

Thackeray thus immortalizes, in "Vanity Fair," the brief connection of William Pitt with Baker Street :—

"Ladies, are you aware that the great Pitt lived in Baker Street? What would not your grandmothers have given to be asked to Lady Hester's (Stanhope's) parties in that now decayed mansion? I have dined in it—*moi qui vous parle.* I peopled the chamber with the ghosts of the mighty dead. As we sat soberly drinking claret with men of to-day, the spirits of the departed came in and took their places at the darksome board. 'The pilot who weathered the storm' tossed off great bumpers of spiritual port; the shade of Dundas did not leave the ghost of a heeltap. Addington sat bowing and drinking in a ghostly way, and was not behindhand when the noiseless bottle went round. Scott, from under bushy eyebrows, winked at the apparition of a bees-wing; Wilberforce's eyes went up to the ceiling as his glass went up full and came down empty. They let the house as a furnished lodging now. Yet Lady Hester once lived in Baker Street, and lies asleep in the wilderness."

The above statement, however, must be taken *cum grano salis*, as the writer was evidently drawing on his imagination, notwithstanding the fact that Pitt had Lord Eldon among his visitors here.

In November, while Pitt was drinking the waters at Bath, a scheme—I will not say a plot—was prepared by George Canning and others of his friends to bring about his return to Downing Street, by signing a sort of "round-robin," suggesting to Mr. Addington the propriety of resigning in his favour; but Mr. Pitt set his foot down upon it most peremptorily, saying that in the eyes of the world such a manifesto would be deemed a Pittite Cabal, and that it would be better to wait the course of events. He was, personally, most anxious for rest and repose. He sought at this date rather to isolate himself from his friends than to increase the number of his followers; and it was a matter of honour with him to lend his entire support to Mr. Addington, so long as he felt that the latter fully appreciated, and was equal to, the difficulties of his position. "It is my wish," he said to Lord Malmesbury, ". . . that no further canvass should be made for names, supporters, or signatures, to promote or compel Mr. Addington's resignation. If my coming into office is as generally desired as you suppose, it is much better for me and for the thing itself to leave that opinion to work out its own way. This must happen if the opinion is a prevailing one in the public mind ; and if it is not, my coming into office at all is useless and improper." Fairer and more straightforward words could not well have been uttered. They were accepted as final by Mr. Pitt's friends, including George Canning, and the project was allowed to drop quietly, though Lord Grenville expressed himself in his private letters to his brother, the Marquis of Buckingham, that the renewal of war with Buonaparte was imminent and unavoidable, and that, if Great Britain wished to resist him successfully, the only hope lay in the return of Pitt to place and power.[1]

In December, Mr. Pitt, while still at Bath, read the published accounts of Addington's Budget. This sadly disappointed and, indeed, annoyed him ; for he saw at a glance that when the new minister expressed an opinion that no fresh taxes would be necessary to meet the probable

[1] See " Courts and Cabinets of George III.," by the Duke of Buckingham, vol. iii. p. 214. Stanhope's " Life of Pitt," vol. iii. p. 76.

expenditure, he did not realize the extreme necessity of being prepared for war.

Mr. Pitt left Bath for London at Christmas, and early in January spent a day with his friend Addington at Richmond Park, when there arose some little misunderstanding between them, which gradually broke out into a real difference. There can be no reasonable doubt that Pitt felt uneasy at being "out of harness," and in his "heart of hearts" longed to return to Downing Street. But having had a hand in placing Addington at the head of the Treasury, and having promised to support him, he could, of course, take no step to regain his lost position. When, however, he came to look into Addington's financial statements, he found, by a glance of his experienced eye, that they did not approve themselves to him ; in fact, that he believed him to have made a miscalculation to the extent of £2,800,000 a year. There is no need to suppose that any bad blood was made between the ex-minister and his successor by any "candid" or uncandid "friend." As Lord Stanhope expresses himself of this "alienation," it was "perfectly consistent, not only with the personal honour and good faith, but also with the public spirit and the friendly inclination of both parties." Their differences arose from causes which might have been foreseen, but which could not be averted. "When a man of moderate abilities is placed at the head of affairs, and when another man of first-rate genius in politics is standing at his side, it must happen that the former will commit some faults which the latter will not be slow to see. A sense of public duty must, in the long run, impel the independent statesman to make known, and, if he can, to correct, if he cannot, to oppose, any great error of the Ministerial measures. Nor can it be avoided, in times of great public danger and affright, that the nation should anxiously turn from the lesser politician to the great one." [1]

The first symptom of actual estrangement appears to have shown itself on the journey to London, when Pitt had a seat

[1] "Life of Pitt," vol. iii. p. 93.

in Addington's carriage. On reaching Hyde Park, we learn from Mr. Rose,[1] Mr. Addington said to him, in a sudden, curt, and embarrassed manner, that if, as he had heard, Lord Grenville had not suggested the necessity of Mr. Pitt's return to Downing Street, "he himself (Mr. A.) should have been disposed to propose his (Mr. P.'s) return to the Administration;" and followed that up in a way which rendered it impossible for Mr. Pitt to remain silent. He therefore said that "whenever it should be thought there was a necessity for his returning to office, he should consider very attentively how far it would be right and proper for him to do so; and in such an event he should first desire to know what His Majesty's wishes might be on the subject, and that he should not decide without knowing the opinion of Mr. Addington and his colleagues about it."

It is clear, from this delay of their discussion till almost the end of the journey, that the subject was one on which Ad-

---

[1] Stanhope's "Life of Pitt," vol. iii. p. 91.

dington was shy of speaking, and that he wished to get over the embarrassing position as quickly as possible.

In the meantime, Mr. Pitt paid visits to Mr. Long on Bromley Hill, and to Lord Camden at Sevenoaks ; and at one or other of these places it is highly probable that one or more of his subordinates helped to fan the fuel of the latent offence into a flame.

Knowing that our relations with France were becoming daily more difficult and perilous, and that any public discussion on points of internal difference at such a moment might make the difference between peace and war, Mr. Pitt thought it best to remain at Walmer, and relinquish for a time his attendance in the House of Commons. He writes at the same time, February, 1803, to his brother, Lord Chatham, that when Mr. Addington brings forward his Budget after Easter, he may possibly be obliged to avoid taking part in debate on it, unless measures should be brought forward very different from those which he then expected, either from what he heard, or from Addington's printed speech. He felt that the insolence and arrogance of Napoleon could be met by nothing short of a strong display of national strength and vigour, and a readiness on the part of the nation to meet the permanent burdens which alone could supply the sinews of war. And on this point he thought that Mr. Addington was not inclined to take those vigorous measures which were necessary in order to preserve peace. In fact, it is clear that Mr. Pitt was disappointed in his nominee or *locum tenens*, as the world thought Addington to be in reality, and that Addington's sensitive nature opened his eyes to the fact that he was despised by his patron for want of vigour.

Meantime Napoleon had not been idle. He had grasped the dominion of both Piedmont and Switzerland, contrary to the spirit of the Treaty of Amiens, and at the same time insisted that England should stand literally by the terms of that Treaty, and cede back Malta to France. News further reached London that fresh arma-

ments on a large scale were being pre-
pared in the ports of both Holland and
France. In a letter to his brother, Lord
Chatham, at this time (March 2nd), Mr.
Pitt writes :—

"We ought to be prepared for the
possibility both of an immediate rupture,
and for his (Napoleon's) following it up,
or rather accompanying it, by attempting
to strike in the first instance some sudden
blow on any vulnerable point. I conclude
this will be so strongly felt that no time
will be lost in putting into immediate
readiness whatever means we possess, and
especially those of floating defences on the
coast, on which so much of our security
against a *coup de main* must depend."

Lord Chatham was at this time a member of Addington's Cabinet. Was it in
consequence of this letter being shown to
the Prime Minister that a message from
the King was read in the House on the
8th of March, announcing these new preparations on part of the First Consul,
and declaring his conviction that "additional measures of precaution" should be

taken forthwith? Be this as it may, the two Houses, as in duty bound, presented loyal addresses, promising the necessary support; the militia were at once called out, and ten thousand men were added to the navy.

Whatever may have been the cause, Mr. Addington did not command the confidence of the country; and the eyes of all turned to the great statesman whom, in spite of the non-success of the army on land, they desired to see again at the helm. Mr. Wilberforce wrote to a friend on the 8th of March: "Pitt's return is talked of and wished." Even Pitt's old enemy, Sir Philip Francis, in the House of Commons drew attention to the fact that in this critical moment "all the eminent ability of England is excluded from the councils of the country. In fair weather," he added, "a moderate share of skill may be sufficient. For the storm that seems to be coming, other pilots should be provided; for if the ship sinks, we must all go down with her."

The ears of Mr. Addington were open

to such words ; and, though doubtless he would have been glad to have resigned the conduct of affairs into the hands of Pitt, yet he had not the courage to carry out his convictions by openly proposing such a step to the King. He halted in a middle and temporizing course, which could not possibly succeed, suggesting that he should himself resign the Treasury, and that Pitt and he should be Secretaries of State, leaving also to Pitt's option the Chancellorship of the Exchequer, Lord Chatham becoming the nominal head of the Ministry, and Mr. Dundas (now Lord Melville[1]) succeeding Lord St. Vincent as First Lord of the Admiralty. But Mr. Pitt declined to have anything to do with such an arrangement, at the same time declaring his opinion that a mere nominal head, who should not be really Prime Minister and enjoy the confidence of the King, would be a source of weakness, not of strength.

[1] He had been raised to the peerage under this title, at Mr. Addington's suggestion, towards the close of the previous year.

At length, finding this to be the case, and patriotically willing to stand aside himself if it were really for the good of the country, Mr. Addington offered to resign, so as to reinstate Pitt in Downing Street, "if in a personal interview their general ideas should be found to coincide."

Mr. J. H. Jesse writes [1] as follows concerning this crisis, so full of misunderstanding in the literal sense of the term :—

" Meantime, while Pitt and Addington had been employed in arranging the *dramatis personæ* of a new Cabinet, the King, deeply interested as he was in the matter, had been kept in the profoundest ignorance of their unconstitutional negotiations. ' It was not,' as Sir George Cornewall Lewis writes, ' a mere question of changing a Cabinet office, as to which a Prime Minister might properly make a preliminary arrangement, subject to the King's confirmation. It was practically a negotiation for a complete alteration of

[1] " Memoirs of the Life of George III.," vol. iii. p. 307.

R

the character of the Government, and the whole discussion proceeded on the assumption that Addington and Pitt were between them to settle who was to be the new Prime Minister.' The King, on being at length informed of what had passed, naturally was extemely hurt and offended with both statesmen. But it was Pitt who, however undeservedly, suffered the most in his estimation. Yet assuredly Pitt was the least to blame of the two. He would scarcely, we imagine, have gone to the lengths which he had done in his treaty with Addington, unless he had believed that the King was privately cognisant of the negotiations."

In like manner Fox wrote to Mr. C. Grey: "Mr. Pitt is, I hear, more and more bitter against the ministers, and feels strongly what he deems the embarrassment of his situation. I am told he even expresses this sentiment—an openness not very usual with him—to some of his friends."[1] And yet, it must be observed,

[1] Jesse's "Memoirs of the Life of George III.," vol. iii. p. 341.

Fox does not speak in any very confident or complimentary terms of the possible return of his rival to place and power. "There is some talk of it," he writes to Lord Lauderdale on April 1st, "but I believe it is all idle. He knows his insignificance, and does not like showing it."

CHAPTER XXI.

PERHAPS there never was a crisis when
the chance of a powerful Ministry was
so hopeful as when Mr. Pitt submitted his
scheme to the King. Fox announced that
he had two conditions on which he insisted,
one of them being that a Coalition was
entirely proper, and the other that no
mediocrities should be admitted into the
Cabinet. The King, during his interview
with Pitt, said that he had intended to
exclude Fox from the Privy Council in
consequence of his action in putting forward as an abstract theory the sovereignty

of the people. In reality, the difference between Pitt and Fox had arisen from the democracy of France, all chance of which, as soon as Napoleon Buonaparte became First Consul, had disappeared ; and a military despotism would have been hardly contended against by both Pitt and Fox. Burke had said of Lord Chatham, that a peep into the King's closet " intoxicated " him; and, in the opinion of Lord John Russell, the son of Lord Chatham, with all his abilities and all his eloquence, seems to have been subject to a similar "intoxication." This, however, is unjust to Pitt, for his perfect sincerity in the matter is beyond question. Although he would not enter into an organized alliance with Fox and the Grenvilles, his formidable attacks on the Addington Administration were none the less weighty by reason of being made single-handed. However, a reconciliation was effected between Pitt and Addington, although the latter felt deeply offended when he was compelled to vacate the Premiership in order to make room for Pitt. Addington's former affection for Pitt had never quite gone, and he felt a somewhat natural desire to return into office, even though he was aware that he could never again attain the high position which he had previously filled. He declared himself to be the party injured, and would not therefore offer the first advances; but he said that if Pitt would only make a slight movement towards a better understanding between them, he would gladly meet him half-way.

But even this did not satisfy the high mind of Pitt. He met Addington at the house of Mr. Charles Long, at Bromley Hill; but he began the interview by saying that " if any change were made, it must be by the King's desire. He must receive, in the first place, His Majesty's express commands, and must hold himself at liberty to submit for His Majesty's consideration a list of persons " with whom he could and would act. He also held himself at liberty to consult with Lord Grenville and Lord Spencer; and he further stipulated that the new arrangement should not be carried out till the negotiations at Paris were ended, and the question of peace or war decided.

It is to the credit of Mr. Addington that he allowed no personal consideration to stand in the way of the public good, and, so far as he was himself concerned, he was willing even to pass away into the obscurity of a Peerage along with the Speakership of the House of Lords, which *pro hac vice* would be severed from the Lord-Chancellorship; but naturally, before coming to a final decision on the matter, he would like to consult his colleagues. They saw objections to serving along with two at least of Pitt's known friends—probably Lord Grenville and Mr. Windham—and so the negotiation was broken off. The King, too, on hearing the details of it, took offence, declared it "a foolish business." Lord Malmesbury, an intimate friend of both Pitt and Addington, declares that in his opinion both parties were in the wrong; whilst, on the contrary, Lord Stanhope is inclined to think that both were in the right. "Both appear to me," he writes,[1] "to have acted with entire rectitude and

---

[1] "Life of Pitt," vol. iii. p. 123.

honour.   Both appear to me to have shown the most scrupulous fidelity to their personal friends.   Pitt cannot be censured for his determination to submit to the King, on again becoming his Prime Minister, a list of the best and ablest Ministry which it was in his power to form.   He would not have fulfilled his bounden duty to his Sovereign had he, in commercial phrase, offered a second-rate article when he might have secured a first-rate.   As little can Addington be blamed for adhering to the principles of his own Government, and seeking to exclude from office, even on strictly public grounds, the statesman who had bitterly opposed and reviled that Government on the great question of peace, and on every other question. . . . The charges of arrogance, then, on Pitt's side, and of duplicity on Addington's, when we examine them, fall alike to the ground."

Meanwhile, time wore on ; Pitt remained at Walmer enjoying the sea breezes and looking after his farm, while the negotiations at Paris were working towards their issue, not a successful one. The French would be content with nothing but the restoration of Malta, for holding back which island there were in the eyes of the First Consul good and sufficient reasons.

It was becoming daily clearer that "a war for the dignity, the independence, the very existence of our nation," to use the words of Macaulay, "was at hand." It came sooner than was actually expected. The ultimatum[1] of England being declined, Lord Whitworth, our ambassador, returned from Paris, and the French Ambassador from London. On the 16th, a message was sent by the King to the Parliament to the effect that negotiations with France were at an end, and that His Majesty appealed with confidence to the public spirit of his brave and loyal subjects; and

[1] The terms were that we should retain Malta for ten years, and then should cede it, not to the Knights, but to the people, another neighbouring island being ceded to us as a naval station ; that England would acknowledge the new Italian States if Holland should be evacuated by the French troops, and sundry stipulations be assented to on behalf of Switzerland and the King of Sardinia.

two days later was published a formal Declaration of War, which was at once echoed back by France, at the instigation, of course, of the First Consul.

War having been thus declared, on the 23rd of May Mr. Pitt appeared once more in the House of Commons, and made one of the finest, if not the finest, of his speeches, on the Address to the King. Such at least is the testimony of those who heard it, for, owing to a mistake on the part of the Speaker, the reporters for the newspapers were excluded. Lord Malmesbury records it in his journal thus :—

"*May* 24.—Pitt's speech last night the finest he ever made. Never was any speech so cheered, or such incessant and loud applause. It was strong in support of war ; but he was silent as to ministers, and his silence either as to praise or blame was naturally construed into negative censure. No one was heard after him." Fox also styled it "a speech which, if Demosthenes had been present, he must have admired, and might have envied." The Address, in spite of the opposition of Fox, Grey, and others, was carried by 398 against 67 votes.

Three days later, Mr. Pitt spoke again, in support of Mr. Fox's proposal to address the King, urging him to accept the mediation of Russia. It is almost needless to add that the mediation was sought and accepted, but that it led to no result.

Though Fox, Sheridan, Grey, and the rest of their party, strongly disapproved of the renewal of the war, yet Lord Macaulay owns that the indignity with which the First Consul had treated England could not have been met in any other way. And, if any stimulus to the war fever was needed on this side of the Channel, that was afforded by a decree issued on May 22nd by the First Consul by which he seized several thousand unoffending Englishmen who happened to be travelling or trading in France, and detained them as prisoners. They were kept in prison at Verdun and elsewhere till the end of the war, and their detention did more than anything else to exasperate the mind of

England against "the Corsican," as he was called in scorn and defiance.

On the 6th of June, when the estimates came on, Pitt assented to the proposal of a new and further levy beyond the ordinary establishment, and also to that of an enrolment of the militia for home defence, and the raising of an army of reserve by ballot. The income tax also was to be renewed under the name of the "Property Duty Bill," some important alterations being made in it by Addington in deference to Pitt's better judgment. Pitt also avowed his opinion of the necessity of defensive works for London.

In the midst of this crisis some temporary excitement was caused by a fresh rising in Ireland, headed by Robert and Thomas Emmett, in which the Chief Justice, Lord Kilwarden, was attacked and killed in the streets. The Habeas Corpus Act was at once suspended in Ireland, and the misguided leaders were arrested, tried by military law, and executed.

The rest of the session was spent in the passing of a large number of individual motions in support of the Ministry, to which Pitt gave at one time a fitful and disdainful support, and at another an opposition, more or less strong, as he thought the occasion demanded. A vote of censure on the ministers, proposed by Colonel Patten, was negatived by a large majority, as was Pitt's proposal " to pass instead to the orders of the day." A similar fate met a vote of censure proposed by Lord Fitzwilliam in the House of Peers ; and the session was prolonged to the middle of August, though little or nothing had been done adequate to the occasion to encounter the designs of Napoleon.

It should be mentioned here, though it forms no portion of the narrative of Mr. Pitt's political life, that early in the April of this year he lost his mother, the venerable Countess of Chatham. She died at Burton Pynsent ; her sons were not summoned to her bedside, or could not travel so far ; and she was buried in the same vault with her husband in Westminster Abbey—the same vault in which Mr. Pitt and his brother, Lord Chatham, were destined to be interred—the one after a lapse of three years, and the other after thirty-three years.

CHAPTER XXII.

NAPOLEON, having sent an army to occupy
Hanover, now made preparations for invading England on a large scale. With
this view he made a camp on the heights
above Boulogne, where a flotilla of ships
was ordered by him to assemble. The
British fleet no doubt commanded the
Channel ; but there were states of wind
and tide when small and light vessels and
flat-bottomed transports could, in the First
Consul's opinion, be brought across, and
could land an army on the flat coast of
Kent. At once the national spirit of

Englishmen was aroused, and in a month the militia was supplemented by whole legions of volunteers, which sprung into existence as if by magic. " The good sense and firmness of the people," to use the words of Sir Walter Scott, " supplied almost all the deficiencies of inexperience. Those who could not serve in person contributed out of their pockets towards the cost, as they foresaw a struggle *pro aris et focis.*" In July the Government brought in a measure for the regulation of the volunteers; and before the end of the summer upwards of 300,000 volunteers were enrolled.

Pitt not only offered to raise a corps of volunteers within the Cinque Ports, but placed himself at its head in person. " By great activity and energy," writes Lord Stanhope, " he had very soon on foot an excellent regiment of volunteers, divided into three battalions and numbering three thousand men. He was constantly seen on horseback and in full volunteer uniform as the colonel in chief, exercising and reviewing his men. It was acknowledged

on all hands that as, from the circumstances of the coast, Pitt held the post of
principal danger, so he set the most conspicuous example of zeal for the national
defence." " Pitt," writes his friend Wilberforce on the 9th of August, "is about to
take the command of three thousand
volunteers as Lord Warden. I am uneasy
at it. He does not engage on equal or
common terms, and his spirit will lead him
to be foremost in the battle ; yet, as it is
his proper post, one can say nothing against
it."

It was felt by all Pitt's friends, and by his
enemies also, that in the event of an invasion he would be exposed to the first blow.
Even Dr. Wolcot, with whose caustic writ-
ings, under the signature of "Peter Pindar,"
many English readers are familiar, wrote
in words of satire, which, properly trans-
lated, imply no small amount of praise :—

"Come the Consul whenever he will,
    And he means it when Neptune is calmer,
  Pitt will send him a d—— bitter pill
    From his fortress the Castle of Walmer."

It is clear that at this time Mr. Pitt

rather overtaxed his physical strength ; and he was glad to welcome his niece, the haughty and eccentric Lady Hester Stanhope,[1] to come and reside him, to keep house and to act as his secretary and amanuensis.

The King reviewed the new volunteers in Hyde Park twice in the course of October, in the presence of an enormous gathering of spectators ; he was much delighted with the sight, as well he might be ; for Lord Eldon, writing many years afterwards, declared it to be " the finest sight that he had ever seen."[2]

Nevertheless, Mr. Pitt was not satisfied with what had been done thus far to resist the threatened invasion.

Early in December he returned to London in order to take part in the discussions which would be sure to arise in the House of Commons, intending, in his own words,

[1] After his death she travelled abroad, and settled down in Mount Lebanon, where she lived a life of seclusion. She died at her Syrian home in June, 1839.

[2] H. Twiss : " Life of Lord Eldon," vol. i. p. 416.

"to notice the principal omissions on the part of Government in providing for our defence, and to suggest the measures which still seem necessary towards completing it." As a matter of fact, the chief "measure" which he suggested was a large increase of the volunteer forces; and here he found no opposition, but on the contrary every support.

The new year opened with several difficulties. First there was the fear of the threatened invasion from Boulogne; secondly, the King was again taken seriously ill; and thirdly, the state of political parties was one of almost hopeless confusion. Pitt was unwilling to take steps to drive the present ministers from office, though much pressed by his friends to do so; he was equally unwilling to enter into a coalition with Fox, as Lord Grenville wished; but he contented himself with watching the course of affairs from a distance, refusing to have a share in any overt act, possibly on account of the continuance of the King's illness. At the same time he did not scruple to tell his private friends that he did not expect the Ministry to last, especially if the King should recover, or on the other hand if he grew worse and a Regency should be appointed. He also gave them to understand that if the King, convinced of the incompetency of his present advisers, should desire him to form a new Ministry, he would do so, selecting its members from his own friends and supporters, including some members of Addington's Cabinet, but excluding both him and Lord St. Vincent.[1]

On the 17th of April Mr. Pitt took part and spoke in the debate on a Bill for the augmentation of the Irish Militia.[2] Horner, who listened to Pitt on this occasion, writes to his father on the following day: " Pitt gave us both substance and manner as a debater of the highest powers. Most explicit in his declaration against ministers, which he delivered, however, as if made

---

[1] See Mr. Pitt's Letter to Lord Melville, March 29, 1804, given in Stanhope's " Life of Pitt," vol. iii. pp. 202–206.

[2] J. H. Jesse's " Memoirs of the Life of George III.," vol. iii. p. 351.

only after much consideration and reluctance; but he enforced it with a good deal of vehement declamation in his way, and some touches of that bitter, freezing sarcasm which everybody agrees is his most original talent, and appears indeed most natural to him."

Toward the end of April, Mr. Addington, finding himself supported in the House of Commons by small and decreasing majorities, tendered his resignation to the King, who had now recovered his mental vigour. The King reluctantly accepted his resignation, at the same time offering to his minister a peerage and a pension— both of which, however, Mr. Addington declined.

On the 30th of the same month Mr. Pitt received, through Lord Eldon, His Majesty's commands to form a new Cabinet. His first wish, as expressed in a communication to the King, was to include in it, not only Lord Grenville, but Fox. The King, however, would not hear of Fox's name being mentioned in connection with a Cabinet office. It was in vain that Pitt urged the necessity of laying aside all thoughts of resentment for past offences in the face of a very present danger ; and at length Pitt agreèd to re-enter the service of the King on condition that Fox, though excluded from the Cabinet, might be employed on a foreign mission should occasion arise. Lord Grenville, however, refused to join any Cabinet from which Fox was excluded.

On the 10th of May Mr. Pitt was enabled to announce to the King, and to obtain His Majesty's approval of, the new Administration, formed mainly out of his own friends and some members of the Cabinet of Mr. Addington; but his own health appears to have been seriously affected by the difficulties, squabbles, and (worst of all) by the misunderstandings of the last few months, and by the feeling that thenceforth he should have to face in Parliament the united forces of the followers of Fox and those of Lord Grenville also. His chief colleagues were Lords Eldon, Chatham, Westmoreland, Hawkesbury, Bathurst, and Melville, and the Dukes of Portland and Montrose, Mr. George

Canning becoming Treasurer of the Navy, but without a seat in the Cabinet.

Mr. Pitt, it should here be stated, had not been at Court for some three years, and had never seen, or at all events had never spoken to, the King during that time. On their meeting, however, the King received Pitt with great cordiality. " I must congratulate your Majesty," said Pitt, "on your looking better now than you did on your recovery from your last illness." "That is not to be wondered at," replied the King : "I was then on the point of parting with an old friend; I am now about to regain one." "Seldom," as Lord Stanhope remarks, " has any sovereign paid a more graceful compliment to any subject."

Still the King, not having entirely recovered from the effects of his recent malady, was much distressed at the break-up of the Addington Ministry. He had always held a high opinion of the late Premier, and he regarded a coalition between Pitt and Fox with feelings of great distrust. He naturally felt under a deep obligation to Addington for having accepted office in the troublous times of 1801, and therefore he was very much displeased with Pitt on account of his action in joining forces with Fox and the Grenvilles in order to oust Addington from his position. He, however, spoke of Pitt in appreciative terms. " I am persuaded," he said, " that Mr. Pitt will never perform any engagement, or enter into any connection, which will be injurious either to the rights of my subjects or to the royal prerogative." The King's chief dread, no doubt, was that of having his old enemy, Fox, forced on him as his personal adviser and confidential minister ; and he regarded the prospect of such an occurrence with much foreboding and displeasure.

On Mr. Pitt resuming office in May, 1804, he saw the camp of Napoleon still on the heights above Boulogne, and the flotilla of boats not yet dispersed. He found the King, however, fairly sane and sound in mind and body, and glad to have once more in his Prime Minister an arm on which he could lean in confidence in times of danger and difficulty. In the same month the First Consul proclaimed himself "Emperor" of France—a step which roused the enmity of half the courts of Europe.

Mr. Pitt found much reason for dissatisfaction at the small and unsatisfactory majorities by which he was supported in his Bill for increasing the army of reserve at the cost of the militia, which had been allowed to grow beyond its normal numbers. But, though his resignation was talked of as imminent, nothing came of it; and in July the parliamentary session was brought to a close, when the King went off to Weymouth for rest and change.

CHAPTER XXIII.

NO sooner was Pitt again installed in office than his friend Wilberforce renewed his motion for the abolition of the slave trade. The question had slept, or perhaps had gone back, in the twelve years that had passed since its first parliamentary success had been gained ; and it had been thrown into the background partly by the events in France, and partly by the opposition of Addington and his party. It was suggested to propose a three years' or five years' suspension of the slave trade; but Wilberforce refused to make a truce with what he held to be a sin, and was cordially supported by Pitt. He carried his Bill through the Commons; but owing to the opposition of the Peers and the lateness of the season, the measure was postponed till the next year. A more vital and more directly practical question was at stake, whether the army should be strengthened at any cost and at all hazards. Pitt desired to reduce the militia, but to increase the army reserves; and in spite of the opposition of all sections of his antagonists, he carried his point in both Houses, though by no very large majorities. A vote of credit for £2,300,000 was also passed without dissent.

At the close of the session Mr. Pitt again repaired to Walmer, and occupied himself in superintending the erection of martello towers along the coast of Kent and Sussex, and the formation of a military canal along the inside of Romney Marsh. It is customary now to laugh at this canal and these towers; but Napoleon in July was actually at Boulogne, and had taken on himself the chief command of his flotilla;

and it was only through the death of one of his admirals and a mistake made by another that the month of July did not witness an attempt to carry out the invasion in full earnest. Indeed, not only at this time, but for ten years more, the proceedings of Napoleon kept the people of England, at all events in the southern and south-eastern counties, in a chronic state of alarm.

Mr. Pitt was mocked at for his precautions as needless and wasteful; but it has been shown from authentic sources by M. Thiers that just at this very moment Napoleon had actually planned the details of his descent on our coast, though at the last moment he had been forced to postpone it for a year. Had Napoleon made the experiment, landed in Romney Marsh, and found his further progress blocked by Pitt's canal, how would the judicious foresight of the Premier have been lauded to the skies!

"Few are alive now," writes Lord Malmesbury, "who have any idea of the excitement which pervaded this country. The

name of Bonaparte was till 1815 the bug-
bear of English mothers and nurses to rule
their wayward children. His name was in
every one's mind, and pronounced with
execration. The country resounded with
the arms of volunteers, yeomanry, and
militia. Every one of our naval successes
and Spanish victories saw the Union Jack
hoisted on the towers of our churches, and
the details, printed in our then scanty
newspapers, were read to shouting crowds
in our market places." [1]

The autumn was largely occupied by a
very delicate business, in which Mr. Pitt's
advice was naturally sought; namely, the
patching up of the family dissensions
between the King and the heir apparent,
and also between the latter and his ill-
mated wife; but little, if any, good resulted
from the interference to which he somewhat
reluctantly consented. It is much, however, to Pitt's honour, that he is credited
by Lord Brougham with having been "the
earliest defender and friend" of that ill-

[1] " Memoirs of an ex-Minister," vol. i. p. 3.

fated lady in this country. It was like Pitt's noble nature to side with the weak and injured party; and though he sought to shield her from her enemies, the more he felt bound to warn her of her faults, and to remonstrate with her on her conduct, especially in her retirement at Blackheath, as disrespectful to the Prince her husband.

In the month of December, through the intervention of the King and one or two mutual friends, the old friendly intercourse between Pitt and Addington was renewed. The peace between the two long-estranged statesmen was ratified in a meeting at Lord Hawkesbury's country seat at Combe Wood on Sunday, the 23rd of December, and on the 26th Mr. Pitt joined Addington's family dinner party. This friendly step approved itself to almost all Pitt's friends, with the exception of George Canning. The result of this pacification was that, a few weeks later (in January, 1805), the Duke of Portland having agreed to retire, Mr. Addington came back into the Cabinet as President of the Council, his great friend Lord Hobart, who had lately become Earl of Buckinghamshire, taking office also as Lord Privy Seal. Mr. Addington was at the same time created Viscount Sidmouth.

We learn from Wilberforce's diary how much pleasure this renewal of the old friendship caused to Pitt; who said to him while walking with him in one of the parks, "I am sure that you are glad to hear that Addington and I are one again. And then," writes Wilberforce, " he added, with a sweetness of manner which I shall never forget, 'I think they are a little hard upon us in finding fault with our making it up again, when we have been friends from our childhood, and our fathers were so before us; while they say nothing to Grenville for uniting with Fox, though they have been fighting all their lives.'"

The man who could speak thus after a quarrel of some years' standing may have been haughty and proud, but can scarcely be thought unfeeling; at all events, he showed that even the post of the First Lord of the Treasury is compatible with a tender and affectionate heart.

CHAPTER XXIV.

Napoleon proposes Peace, but is refused—Pitt and the Archbishopric of Canterbury—Pitt's Last Budget—Impeachment of Lord Melville —Pitt again visits Addington at Richmond Park—Their Last Meeting.

EARLY in this year the Emperor Napoleon addressed to the King of England a letter, couched in general terms, desiring to make peace ; " but," writes Lord Stanhope, " so much were particulars avoided, that, in the judgment of Mr. Pitt and his colleagues, this overture was designed for popular effect rather than for positive negotiation." The reply sent in His Majesty's name declared that the King had most sincerely at heart the object of peace, but that in arranging it he must act in concert with his allies on the Continent, and especially with the Russian Emperor.

About this time the death of Dr. Moore, Archbishop of Canterbury, placed at the disposal of the King a prize which Mr. Pitt naturally wished to have conferred on his friend and former tutor, Dr. Tomline, Bishop of Lincoln. But the King forestalled Pitt's application by promising it, as soon as he heard the news, to Dr. Manners Sutton, Dean of Windsor and Bishop of Norwich; and Mr. Pitt was obliged to yield, though not, it is said, without having first used some very strong words of remonstrance to His Majesty. Indeed, Lord Sidmouth is said to have expressed to the late Dean Milman his belief that "such strong language had hardly ever passed before between a sovereign and his minister."

The session was opened by the King in person, and no amendment to the usual address was moved; though Fox expressed great dissatisfaction that nothing had been done to conciliate the Roman Catholics by any mention of a repeal of their disabilities; and Mr. Grey sought, but unsuccessfully, to censure the conduct of the war against Spain. Mr. Pitt made in March one of his most brilliant speeches against a motion of Sheridan to repeal the Additional Force Bill. The motion was rejected by a large majority; but when Sheridan declared that Mr. Pitt by his conduct had " merited the contempt and execration of all good men," there were those who feared that another duel on Wimbledon Common would be the consequence. The threatened thunderstorm, however, blew over, and a week or two afterwards Pitt found himself in the same lobby with Fox and Sheridan also in support of a motion to postpone, as ill-timed, Mr. Wilberforce's renewal of his Anti-Slavery Bill. In February he brought forward that Budget which was destined to be his last. He had to provide for the estimates, and also for a possible subsidy, amounting in all to forty-four millions. To meet this, it would be necessary, Mr. Pitt said, to continue all the war taxes, including the property tax, and to contract a new loan of twenty millions more; and to meet the interest on the loan, it would be necessary to impose fresh taxes to the extent of yet another million. Mr. Pitt accordingly proposed an addition to the charge on letters sent by post, to the duties on salt and on horses of every kind, and an increase in the legacy duties. But these, and also his Supplemental Budget, he contrived to carry, so firmly was he established in the confidence of the nation.

Almost the last speech of Mr. Pitt in the House of Commons was in his own defence against a motion of Mr. Samuel Whitbread censuring him for having advanced £40,000 of public money to Messrs. Boyd, Benfield & Co., without insisting on adequate security being taken. His own conduct, he said in reply, "though irregular, was both reasonable and expedient;" and so paramount was his influence that a Bill of indemnity was afterwards passed in his favour.

But about this time another cause of great disquietude and pain arose; for Mr. Whitbread suddenly gave notice of a hostile inquiry into some acts of mal-administration of which Lord Melville had been guilty in the person of his subordinates at the Admiralty Board. This was based on a Report by the Commissioners of Naval Inquiry, which showed that some moneys in the hands of a Mr. Alexander Trotter, Paymaster of the Navy under his Lordship, had been misapplied, having been probably mixed up with some Secret Service money at home or abroad. No doubt there had been laxity in the department, but nothing of a criminal nature was proved. Still, a shaft aimed successfully at Lord Melville, his adversaries knew, would strike deep into the proud heart of his friend Mr. Pitt, and at all events would help to embarrass his Ministry.

Pitt moved the previous question, and he was supported by a new member, Lord Henry Petty, afterwards Marquis of Lansdowne ; but he had the mortification of being opposed by his great personal friend, Wilberforce, and further of finding the members equal on a division, when the Speaker gave his casting vote in favour of the censure of Lord Melville. Thus condemned, Lord Melville resigned office, though he lost but little of the esteem of his friends, and lived in high honour for several years in the retirement of his Scottish home. His place at the Admiralty was filled by an admiral little known to fame up to that time,—Sir Charles Middleton, who was created Lord Barham.

But the blow fell heavily on Pitt. One of the country squires who sat with him in St. Stephen's, on hearing the result of the debate, cried out in delight, "We have killed the fox;" but whether he meant Pitt or Melville, is not quite certain. If he meant the former, he had the satisfaction of finding his words verified literally in a very few months.

Mr. Pitt could not well omit to speak on the impeachment of his old friend. The substance of his speech, however, was to the effect that an impeachment, in such cases, is to be preferred to a criminal prosecution in the ordinary courts of law, as offering less chance of delay, and ensuring a fuller investigation of the charges alleged.

On this occasion, an amendment moved by Mr. Fox having been negatived, the motion for Lord Melville's impeachment was carried without a division. It was ordered " that Mr. Whitbread do go to the Lords, and, at their bar, in the name of the House of Commons of the United Kingdom of Great Britain and Ireland, impeach Henry Viscount Melville of high crimes and misdemeanours, and acquaint them that this House will in due time exhibit particular articles against him, and make good the same."

This step, and the erasure of Lord Melville's name from the list of Her Majesty's Privy Council, which he had been forced to advise the King to sanction, followed by Napoleon's great victory at Austerlitz, may be said to have combined to kill Mr. Pitt, whose haughty yet sensitive nature was not proof against such blows.

" I have ever thought," writes Lord Fitzharris[1] in his note-book, " that an aid-

---

[1] Afterwards second Earl of Malmesbury.

ing cause of Pitt's death, certainly one that tended to shorten his existence, was the result of the proceedings against his old friend and colleague, Lord Melville. I sat wedged close to Pitt himself the night we were left 216 to 216, and the Speaker, Abbot, after looking as white as a sheet, and pausing for ten minutes, gave the casting vote against us. Pitt immediately put on the little cocked hat which he was in the habit of wearing when dressed for the evening, and jammed it deeply over his forehead ; and I distinctly saw the tears trickling down his cheeks."

During the protracted proceedings against his friend and colleague, Pitt had experienced an anxious and a sorrowful time. He knew that the impeachment of Lord Melville would probably break up his Administration, and the uncertain and unhappy fate of one who had been his intimate companion and warm adherent in many a well-fought parliamentary contest caused him the deepest pain. His weak state of health, combined with the fatigues of office, began to have a baneful influence upon his nervous system, and made him unfit to support the blow. Lord Barham's appointment to the Admiralty all but led to the resignation of Lord Sidmouth, and of his *alter ego*, Lord Buckinghamshire ; but they were induced, at the urgent desire of Mr. Pitt, to reconsider and withdraw that step.

Happily the political connection between Addington and Pitt closed in a more satisfactory manner to both of them than might have been expected. At a meeting which took place between them on the 6th of July, at Pitt's villa on Putney Heath, scarcely six months before the death of the great minister, they parted not only on friendly but on affectionate terms. " Has there been anything in my conduct at any time," asked Lord Sidmouth, " inconsistent with what was due to a friend ? " "Never," was Pitt's reply ; at the same time, with tears standing in his eyes, taking the other's hand, " I have nothing to acknowledge from you but the most generous and honourable conduct, and I am grieved that we are to part." When, at the end of

September, Lord Sidmouth happened to be borne down by family affliction and bodily disease, Pitt paid him a visit at his lodge in Richmond Park, where the two friends friends once more met and parted in kindness. It was destined that they should never meet again.[1]

[1] See J. H. Jesse's "Memoirs of George III.," vol. iii. p. 439.

CHAPTER XXV.

Pitt meets Sir Arthur Wellesley and Lord Nelson—Pitt's Firm Opposition to Napoleon —First Symptoms of Serious Illness—He is cheered by the News of the Victory at Trafalgar, but crushed by that of the Defeat at Austerlitz—Goes to Bath—Grows worse—Returns to his Home at Putney Heath—His Death—His Funeral in Westminster Abbey.

WE have now for the first time brought before us the name of the great Duke of Wellington, who saw the great statesman in the flesh when he was at the very close of his career. *Virgilium vidit tantum.*

"Early in September Sir Arthur Wellesley arrived in London, fresh from the early laurels which he had gained in India, and brought with him a letter of strong recommendation to Pitt from his brother, Lord Wellesley, then Governor General of that distant dependency. Sir Arthur, on his arrival in England, was most warmly welcomed by Mr. Pitt, both as the brother of a constant friend, and as himself the victor of Assaye and Argaum. They had many conversations on military matters, and each made a favourable impression on the other. The Duke of Wellington, to the close of his life, continued to speak of Mr. Pitt in terms of high regard and veneration. He used, during several years, to attend the anniversaries of the Pitt Dinner, with the object of doing honour to his memory ; and he has more than once told me that, in his opinion, Mr. Pitt was the greatest minister that has ever ruled in England." [1]

During the autumn, though he felt increasing illness, Mr. Pitt did not relax his vigilance against the great enemy of Great Britain, the Emperor Napoleon. On the contrary, at the beginning of October we find him at Walmer Castle, intent upon a scheme for destroying the French boats which remained at Boulogne. Soon after

[1] Lord Stanhope's " Life of Pitt," vol. iii. p. 353.

this date, however, he returned to his villa on Putney Common, where he learned the news of the Emperor Napoleon's victory at Ulm. The intelligence caused a great shock to Mr. Pitt's nervous system; and the news of Lord Nelson's victory at Trafalgar, which arrived four days later, only partially revived him.

Mr. Pitt spent the rest of the autumn partly in London, partly at Putney, and partly in visiting some of his intimate friends—Lord Camden at the Wilderness, and Lord Bathurst at Cirencester; and he dined at the Lord Mayor's feast at the Guildhall on the 9th of November, Sir Arthur Wellesley being another guest. When the Lord Mayor proposed his health as one who "had been the saviour of England and would be the saviour of Europe," Mr. Pitt rose, disclaimed the compliment for himself, and briefly said, "England has saved herself by her own exertions, and the rest of Europe will be saved by her example." According to the Duke of Wellington's testimony, given verbally in after-years to Lord Stanhope, "that was all; he was scarcely up for two minutes, yet nothing could be more perfect." It was his last speech, and, indeed, his last appearance in public.

On that very morning he had written to the family of Lord Nelson, announcing that on account of the splendid victory, in the midst of which the gallant admiral had fallen, an earldom with a pension would be bestowed on his successors.

On the 7th of December, Mr. Pitt left London for Bath, only to return from it a month later a dying man. Yet here, ill as he was, he received visits from Lord Hawkesbury, Lord Mulgrave, and Lord Melville. He was here when he received the news of the utter defeat of the Russians and Austrians by Napoleon at Austerlitz, and the cession of the Tyrol and the Venetian territory at his bidding. That news dealt Mr. Pitt his death-blow.

Had he been spared to return in health to meet Parliament in the following month, there is little doubt that his Ministry would have stood, for had he not Trafalgar to set against Ulm and Austerlitz? But such was not his fate. *Dis aliter visum.* His body was enfeebled by the gout, and though he was able to write a letter to Lord Castlereagh on the 6th, and another to Lord Stanhope on the 8th of January, these were the last efforts of a dying man. He was joined at Bath by his friend and physician, Sir Walter Farquhar, who, with Mr. Charles Stanhope, on the 9th accompanied him on his last journey towards his home at Putney. He was three days upon the road ; and when he arrived, his niece, Lady Hester Stanhope, saw an alarming change in his appearance. Nevertheless, on the 13th, and again on the 14th, he was able to take short carriage drives ; but he never left his house afterwards. He received visits from Lord Wellesley and from his brother, Lord Chatham, as well as from Mr. George Rose, Lord Hawkesbury, and Bishop Tomline, who prayed by his bedside. He was able to sign his will ; and early on Thursday, the 23rd of January, he breathed his last, his last words being, according to Mr. James H. Stanhope, "Oh ! my country ! how I leave—or how I love—

my country!" for there is a doubt as to the exact word used.

Mr. Pitt expired on the twenty-fifth anniversary of the day on which he first set foot in the House of Commons. On the 20th and 21st of February his remains lay in state in the Painted Chamber at Westminster. At the interment the pall-bearers were the Archbishop of Canterbury, and the Dukes of Portland, Beaufort, and Montrose. Among those who walked in the procession were the Speaker of the House of Commons, the Lord Mayor of London, thirty-two peers, including three princes of the blood, ten bishops, and about one hundred and fifty members of the House of Commons. The chief mourner was the Earl of Chatham, and he was supported by six gentlemen, all of whom either had been or were afterwards prime ministers of England : Lord Sidmouth, Lord Grenville, Spencer Perceval, Lord Liverpool, George Canning, and Sir Arthur Wellesley. The body of Pitt was interred in the grave of his illustrious father. The titles of the deceased having been proclaimed, the herald pronounced over the grave the not unmerited eulogium, *Non sibi sed patriæ vixit*, and the memorable ceremony concluded.

The King was so overcome by the news of the death of his favourite minister, that he could not bear to speak of the event or to see any of his other ministers for two or three days, and it was feared by many that the effect on the royal mind would be disastrous. His Majesty had little faith in Lord Sidmouth's capacity as the head of a Government ; and when he applied to Lord Hawkesbury to form an Administration, that astute statesman contented himself with securing the Lord Wardenship of the Cinque Ports, and declined to enter into the difficulties with which even Pitt had been unable to cope.

CHAPTER XXVI.

*Memorials of Pitt—Testimonies to his Public
Character—His Private Character: Fondness for Country Pursuits ; his Learning ;
his Popularity among Friends—Pitt as an
Orator—Lecky's Estimate of him—Conclusion.*

AT his death in 1806, Mr. Pitt had no
surviving near relative except his elder
brother, the Earl of Chatham. His sisters
had both died in early womanhood, soon
after their respective marriages. His
younger sister, Lady Harriet Eliot, left
an only child, Hester Harriet Pitt, who
afterwards became the wife of Lieut.-
General Sir William H. Pringle.

His elder sister, Lady Hester, Countess
Stanhope, left at her decease, in 1780,
three daughters, Lady Hester Stanhope—
the eccentric and haughty Queen of the
Eastern Desert — who lived unmarried,

and died in 1839; Lady Griselda Jekyll, who lived on till 1851; and Lady Lucy Rachel Taylor, who died in 1814. Lord Chatham, his elder brother, though a general and once a Cabinet Minister, had passed away out of public recollection long before his death at Brighton in the autumn of 1835. He died childless, and the earldom became extinct. His decease is briefly and cynically mentioned by Mr. C. Greville in his Memoirs[1] as "of no other importance than that of giving some honours and emoluments for Lord Melbourne to distribute." Alas! how unlike the national excitement which was caused by the first Lord Chatham's death, some sixty years before!

The name of Pitt has been to some extent immortalized by the Pitt University Press at Cambridge, and by a Pitt Club, which has been supposed to keep up the tradition of his opinions, though we have seen these to have been far different from those with which the Toryism of Lords

---

[1] 1st Series, iii. 316, Note.

Eldon and Liverpool had much affinity. His old friend the Duke of Richmond was the first President of this club, which for many years celebrated the great statesman's birthday by a triennial dinner, either at the London Tavern or at Merchant Taylors' Hall; and the club still holds two dinners yearly. The badge of membership was a gilt medal on a lozenge-shaped ground of black enamel, with the legend—"*Non sibi sed patriæ vixit.*"

A grand and sumptuous monument, at the public cost, was erected to Pitt's memory in Westminster Abbey, not far from that of his illustrious father, and near that of his rival Fox—a monument which is all the better known to the public on account of Sir Walter Scott's celebrated lines in his Preface to "Marmion":—

> "Nor mourn ye less his perish'd worth,
> Who bade the conqueror go forth,
> And launch'd that thunderbolt of war
> On Egypt, Hafnia, Trafalgar;
> Who, born to guide such high emprize,
> For Britain's weal was early wise;
> Alas! to whom th' Almighty gave,
> For Britain's sins, an early grave!

> His worth, who, in his mightiest hour,
> A bauble held the pride of power,
> Spurn'd at the sordid lust of pelf,
> And served his Albion for herself.
>   *   *   *   *   *
> Oh ! think, how to his latest day,
> When Death, just hovering, claim'd his prey,
> With Palinure's unalter'd mood,
> Firm at his dangerous post he stood ;
> Each call for needful rest repell'd,
> With dying hand the rudder held,
> Till in his fall, with fateful sway,
> The steerage of the realm gave way !
>   *   *   *   *   *
> While faith and civil peace are dear,
> Grace this cold marble with a tear—
> He, who preserved them, Pitt, lies here !

A statue of Pitt, "lean, arrogant, and with the nose on which he 'dangled the Opposition' sufficiently prominent," to use the words of Macaulay, was erected, in 1812, in Hanover Square, from the designs of Bubb, the sculptor, at a cost of a little over £4,000. Pitt stands on a rock, dressed as the Chancellor of the Exchequer, and below him stand Apollo and Mercury, as representatives of Eloquence and Learning. The inscription was written by George Canning.

It is impossible to conclude even so brief a memoir of one of our greatest statesmen without adding a few general remarks on his character, both public and private. There is no doubt that he was neither a Tory nor a Whig, neither what would now be called a Conservative nor a Liberal, for those terms in a century have come very largely to have changed their meaning. He was *sui generis;* if anything, a "Chathamite." He soared above party, and, at all events till enslaved by the King, he viewed all measures with a patriotic eye, and judged them by the patriot's only standard—will they, or will they not, work for the good, not of this or that section, but of the country and the state at large? If anything, he was of Tory descent, his first chief, Lord Shelburne, and his father, Lord Chatham, having both inherited their political opinions from Lord Bolingbroke, and certainly having been always opposed to the oligarchy of "the great Whig families," who had monopolized place and power ever since the reign of William the Third.

Mr. Pitt's public career naturally divides itself into two distinct parts, the first extending from his accession to the post of Premier in December, 1783, to February 1793, when he declared war against France and during which he was a strong Liberal, though certainly not a Radical; and the second reaching from the latter date until he quitted Downing Street in 1801, or rather down to his death, and during which period he was as certainly a professed Tory. He may have been during this second period "the pilot that weathered the storm"; but he was a pilot who, while he showed skill in avoiding the rocks and shoals on which the good ship Britannia might have been wrecked, stood more aghast at those dangers than was necessary, and needlessly altered her course in consequence.

Lord Beaconsfield used to say that during the former period, as well as the latter, Pitt was a genuine Tory; but Macaulay avows that "at this period he was a better Whig than even Charles James Fox." "These conflicting opinions," remarks Mr. Kebbel, "form a curious illustration of what Pitt said himself—that he belonged to neither party."

Mr. Kebbel holds that Pitt's principles, even at this date, were Tory; but he seems to identify Toryism with the dictum that "the King has a right to choose his own ministers." "But," he adds, "Pitt's measures were Liberal in every sense of the word. Free Trade, Parliamentary Reform, the French Alliance, and Relief to Roman Catholics: these were all his favourite ideas." But not every reader will follow him when he says further that these measures were "characteristic of the Tories," and "conceived in accordance with the traditions of Toryism." For, it may be asked, what are measures except principles carried out into practice? At all events, that is what they ought to be; and a disagreement between the two looks very much like hypocrisy.

Pitt's public character is thus drawn by his friend Wilberforce in 1798 :—

"It is my deliberate judgment, formed on much experience and close observation, that Pitt has more disinterested patriotism and a purer mind than almost any man, not under the influence of Christian principles, I ever knew. That he has weaknesses and faults I freely confess, but a want of ardent zeal for the public welfare and of the strictest love of truth are not of the number. I speak not this from the partiality of personal affection ; in fact, for several years past there has been so little of the *eadem velle* and *eadem nolle*, that friendship has starved for want of nutriment. I really love him for his public qualities and his private ones, though there too he is much misunderstood."

Mr. Pitt showed the extent of his influence over the mind of George III. by the number of peerages which were created during the twenty years of his Premiership. It is quite true that no one was raised to a dukedom on his recommendation ; but the ranks of English marquises were increased by him from one to twelve in England, and to nine in Ireland. At his death in 1806, there were twenty-seven English earls and twenty-eight Irish earls, eight English and thirteen Irish viscounts, seventy-four English and forty-six Irish barons, besides fifteen peeresses in their own right, all created subsequent to 1783, and for all of which creations, except four or five that belong to Lord Sidmouth, Mr. Pitt was responsible. In other words, he increased the peerage of the United Kingdom by one-third.

In proof of the permanence of the influence which he exercised as a Parliamentary reformer, it may be mentioned that his name was brought, many years after his death, to the front of the battle waged by Sir Francis Burdett, Lord John Russell, and the other disciples of Fox, against the abuses of close boroughs and of cities without the franchise. In July, 1819, Sir Francis Burdett spoke thus : " Many years ago Mr. Pitt had declared a reform in the representation to be absolutely necessary. He had said that in the then present state of the representation no honest man could conduct public affairs, and, in fact, no honest man could be minister ; and he predicted that without a reform the country would be plunged into new wars, undertaken, like the American War, for the purpose of extinguishing liberty in whatever quarter of the world it should appear."[1] It will not be forgotten that even as late as the resignation of the Addington Administration, his opponents, with Fox at their head, were not unwilling to enter into a coalition with him ; and this in itself is a proof that in the eyes of his contemporaries he was still identified with the cause of Constitutional Reform, though he declined to bring it forward at an inconvenient season.

The student of Aristotle, as he reads Pitt's life, can hardly fail to be reminded of the μεγαλόψυχος—the man of truly great soul, "who deems himself worthy of great things, himself being worthy of them." Pitt thus speaks of himself, for instance, in the debate of June 18th, 1804 : "It surely will not be considered that it is no change that the office of the First Lord of the Treasury, reckoned that which has a leading

---

[1] "Annual Register," 1819, p. 247.

influence in the executive government, is now held by *me*. Few will doubt that a very great change has taken place." It can hardly be supposed that Pitt meant to imply that the change had been for the worse. In fact, during the last few years of his life, he appears to approach very closely to the Pompey of Lucan's " Pharsalia " :—

"Nec quisquam perferre potest, Cæsarve priorem
    Pompeiusve parem. . . ."

The oratory of Pitt has often been compared with that of his rival, Fox. It is thus contrasted by Sir N. W. Wraxall: "It is not easy to decide as to their respective superiority in eloquence. Fox's oratory was more impassioned ; Pitt could boast greater correctness of diction : the former exhibited, while speaking, all the Tribunitian rage; the latter displayed the Consular dignity." But then it must be remembered that Fox, of necessity, had more often to speak in attack, while Pitt seldom spoke except in defence ; and the former duty affords greater scope for oratory than the latter. " To Pitt's speeches," remarks

Wraxall, who constantly heard him in Parliament, " nothing seemed wanting, yet there was no redundancy. He seemed, as by intuition, to hit the precise point, where, having attained his object, as far as eloquence could attain it, he sat down. . . . Indeed, so well was the relative proportion of time generally taken up by the two speakers known to the older members, that they calculated that, whenever Fox was three hours on his legs, Pitt replied in two." " Pitt's eloquence was ' matchless,' " writes his friend and tutor, Bishop Tomline ; " such was the uninterrupted flow of his eloquence, without hesitation or repetition, as to render it peculiarly difficult to report his speeches with correctness." Lord Holland, however, used to express his belief that the younger Pitt was not so eloquent as his father had been, and Grattan said much the same : " he takes longer flights, but does not soar so high." [1]

Pitt's great superiority to his antagonist, Fox, and his consequent ministerial success,

---

[1] See Greville's " Memoirs," 1st S., iii. 131.

according to Sir N. W. Wraxall, flowed from his admirable judgment and prudence, which led him to spare the King, and to avoid bringing his name into debate, whilst attacking his ministers during the American War. That same prudence also led him to decline accepting office as Prime Minister on Lord Shelburne's resignation, though pressed to do so by the King, and to content himself with biding his time and reducing Fox's majority in the Commons. In the same spirit of prudence, in opposition to Fox and his friends, he advised the Heir Apparent to accept the Regency on conditions, instead of claiming it as a right. " The minister instantly perceived, and fastened like an eagle on his adversary's error; and this, by producing delay, happily allowed time for the King's recovery, and, of course, perpetuated the duration of Pitt's power." [1]

Still, in spite of his wisdom, Pitt was occasionally at fault, and unable to read the signs of the times. A very striking

---

[1] Sir N. W. Wraxall's " Memoirs," ii. 288.

instance of this want of foresight is related of him by Mr. J. Harford, in his " Recollections of Wilberforce." He tells us that " Pitt considered that the French War, into which he said that he was forced, would be over in a twelvemonth.[1] Burke took a different view. . . . I remember another mistaken anticipation of Pitt's. It seems to me but yesterday that he said in my hearing, that, though it might be presumption in him to point out the very *day* on which it would be impossible for the French Government, beggared as he knew it to be in its resources, to go on, he would almost venture to name the *week*. This statement was made just a fortnight before Marengo." So true was the estimate formed concerning him by Addington, that he was " the most sanguine of men."

How Pitt collected his mass of knowledge no one ever knew. He certainly did not gain it through foreign travel. We learn, on Addington's authority, that " he

---

[1] On one occasion Mr. Pitt mentioned a still shorter period ; namely, " by Easter."

was hardly ever seen with a book in his hand after his accession to power, sat late at table, and never rose till eleven, and then generally took a short ride in the park. He must therefore have extracted information from those he conversed with, as plants imbibe nutriment from the air around them."[1]

Yet certainly he had no great taste for general literature; and throughout his life there are few traces of his having cared to become acquainted with men of letters. Even of Gibbon there is scarcely any mention in Mr. Pitt's life, though the historian's great friend, Lord Sheffield, was a constant visitor at the hospitable house of Pitt's own friend, Lord Auckland, who was his neighbour at Beckenham.

In consequence of this want of taste and mental culture, Pitt showed one great fault as a minister. He cared little or nothing for the claims of art, science, or literature. Like Horace Walpole, he ignored every world except that in which his lot was

---

[1] Pellew's " Life of Sidmouth," vol. ii. p. 152.

cast.   No poet, no historian, no scholar, no man of letters, no artist, painter, or sculptor, owed anything to Pitt's encouragement or patronage.   So far as he was concerned, they might have starved ; and, to use Macaulay's scathing words, "no ruler whose abilities and attainments would bear any comparison with his own, has ever shown such cold disdain for what is excellent in arts and letters."

And yet the kind and generous dictates of Pitt's heart were such as to enlist him on the side of the slaves, when the question of African and West Indian slavery was fairly brought before the House of Commons by his early friend, William Wilberforce.   It was in concert with Mr. Pitt that the latter undertook the work of carrying the Act for their emancipation ; and finally, as we have seen, it was whilst seated on a bench beneath a tree at the hospitable house of Mr. Pitt, at Holwood, that Wilberforce avowed to the sympathetic ears of the great statesman his intention to carry a measure for the abolition of slavery through the British Parliament and to devote, if necessary, his whole life to that sacred cause.

Pitt's character was not without other defects. Brought up in private, he knew but little of mankind, except in the House of Commons; he was but slightly acquainted with the hidden springs of action in human nature at large; and, except to a few chosen intimate friends and associates, he was haughty, distant, and ungenial. He started with large and liberal ideas and hopes and purposes; but these he too readily abandoned at the dictation of the King; and the distant thunders of tumult and outbreak in a neighbouring country caused in him a revulsion of feeling and a reaction of conduct which must have surprised alike his friends and his foes.

Passing from his public to his private life, we find an almost complete consensus of those who knew him as to his personal goodness and worth, and to his social qualities. His career at Cambridge was spotless, and even austere in its morality, and he seems to have maintained the same character through life; indeed, it was observed, with something like a sneer by Sir N. W. Wraxall and others of his contemporaries, that he was the only great minister of the Crown since the days of Elizabeth who lived and died unmarried.

Pitt was very fond of the country, and of rural pursuits. Holwood was to him a second "Sabine farm." He loved to retreat from town and business to that quiet, homelike spot, where he amused his leisure hours by planting, as his father had done at Hayes; and he was never so happy as when he had Wilberforce, Dundas, or Addington staying with him there.

He was also fairly fond of reading, though not a great student, even of the classics; but he knew these well enough to be able to quote them occasionally with great effect in the House of Commons. As we have seen, however, he was wonderfully well informed on general subjects, both in history and in politics, on which he had perhaps thought even more than he had read; though it is on record that, in order to gain his mastery of finance, he read several times over Adam Smith's "Wealth of Nations."

"Several testimonies which I have already cited," writes Lord Stanhope,[1] "speak of Mr. Pitt in his earlier years as a most delightful companion, abounding in wit and mirth, and with a flow of lively spirits. As the cares of office grew upon him, he went, of course, much less into general society. He would often for whole hours sit or ride with only Steele, or Rose, or Dundas for his companion. Nor was this merely for the ease and rest of thus unbending his mind. Men who know the general habits of great ministers are well aware how many details may be expedited and difficulties smoothed away by a quiet chat with a thoroughly trusted friend in lesser office. Pitt, however, often gave and accepted small dinner parties, and took great pleasure in them.

"The testimony of his familiar friend, Lord Wellesley, which goes down to 1797, is most strong upon these points. 'In all

---

[1] "Life of Pitt," vol. i. p. 197.

places, and at all times,' he writes, 'his constant delight was in society. There he shone with a degree of calm and steady lustre which often astonished me more than his most splendid efforts in Parliament. His manners were perfectly plain ; his wit was quick and ready. He was endowed beyond any man of his time whom I knew with a gay heart and a social spirit.' "

It has been the fashion to speak of Mr. Pitt as wanting in the cardinal virtue of sobriety ; but it must be remembered that he lived in a day when every gentleman was supposed to drink his bottle of port daily ; and there is no evidence to support the opposite view, except the fact that once, and only once, he and his friend Dundas appeared in the House in a state of insobriety—namely, on a debate upon Lord Howe's promotion.

He would generally swallow a bottle of port wine before joining in any debate ; and Sir N. W. Wraxall tells us that on one occasion the Minister and his Treasurer of the Navy came down to the House " after a repast not of a Pythagorean description," and "found themselves unable to manage the debate." He adds: "No illiberal notice or advantage was, however, taken of this solitary act of indiscretion. The House broke up, and it sunk into oblivion."

After the debates were over, Pitt would often step in to sup with his friend the Speaker, Addington, who used to say to him, "Now, Pitt, you have had enough; you shall not have another drop." Pitt often promised that if another bottle were sent for, he would take only one glass; but this promise was as often broken as kept.

Mr. Lecky is at great pains to show, in his "History of England," that Pitt was all the more likely to become a successful statesman because he had about him no great original genius, though he possessed many of the secondary qualities in an extraordinary degree. Hence, he holds, arose his great success, which, in some respects, resembled that of Walpole, Peel, and Palmerston, and which enabled him to preserve his hold both on the King and on the nation to the day of his death. According to Mr. Lecky, Pitt was "excellent as a parliamentary debater, and he found his true *rôle* on the arena of the House of Commons. He had a fine voice and commanding presence; a great flow of words, a lucid style, and a power of arranging his thoughts in unpremeditated debate; but he never rose into the higher flights of oratory like his father. Those who read his speeches," writes Mr. Lecky, "will derive little from them but disappointment. What especially strikes the reader is their extreme poverty of original thought. They are admirably adapted to their immediate purpose, but beyond that they are almost worthless. It has been said with truth that not one philosophical remark, not one image, not even one pointed aphorism out of them, has been remembered. There is not a trace in them of the wide or subtle political views, the exquisite delineations of character, the deep insight into the springs of human feeling and action, which make the speeches of Burke so invaluable.

Burke himself once described Pitt with much bitterness as 'the sublime of mediocrity.' . . . Hardly any other great speaker was or is so little remembered, and the few phrases which are not forgotten are only instances of the happy expression of perfectly commonplace ideas."

" Pitt," concludes Mr. Lecky, was "a politician and nothing more. Office to him was the all in all of life ;—not its sordid fruits, for to these he was wholly indifferent ; not the opportunity which it gives of advocating and advancing great causes—for this he cared much too little ; but the excitement and exultation which the possession and skilful exercise of power can give, was to him the highest of pleasures. It was, as he truly said, the pride of his heart and the pleasure of his life. Parliamentary talents under a parliamentary government are often extravagantly over-rated, and the type which I have endeavoured to describe, though combining great qualities of both intellect and character, is not, I think, of the very highest order. Under such a government, Pitt was, indeed, pre-eminently formed to be a leader of men, capable alike of directing, controlling, and inspiring, of impressing the imagination of nations, of steering the bark of the State in times of great difficulty and danger. He was probably the greatest of English parliamentary leaders; he was one of the greatest of parliamentary debaters; he was a very considerable finance minister, and he had a sane, sound judgment of ordinary events. But his eye seemed always fixed on the immediate present or on the near future. His mind, though quick, clear, and strong, was narrow in its range, and neither original nor profound; and though his nature was pure, lofty, and magnanimous, there were moral as well as mental defects in his statesmanship. Of his sincere and single-minded patriotism there can, indeed, I believe, be no doubt."[1]

[1] "History of England," vol. v.

FINIS.

www.ingramcontent.com/pod-product-compliance
Lightning Source LLC
Chambersburg PA
CBHW031025120726
47905CB00007B/2051